White Bread Competition

Jo Ann Yolanda Hernández

PIÑATA
BOOKS

PIÑATA BOOKS
HOUSTON, TEXAS
1997

This volume is made possible through grants from the National Endowment for the Arts (a federal agency), Andrew W. Mellon Foundation, the Lila Wallace-Reader's Digest Fund and the City of Houston through The Cultural Arts Council of Houston, Harris County.

Piñata Books are full of surprises!

Piñata Books
A Division of Arte Público Press
University of Houston
Houston, Texas 77204-2090

Cover illustration and design by Gladys Ramirez

Hernández, Jo Ann Yolanda.
    White bread competition / by Jo Ann Yolanda Hernández.
      p.   cm.
    Summary: When Luz, a ninth-grade Latina student in San Antonio, wins a spelling competition, her success triggers a variety of emotions among family, friends, and the broader community.
    ISBN 1-55885-210-7 (pbk. : alk. paper)
    1. Mexican Americans--Juvenile fiction. [1. Mexican Americans--Fiction. 2. Competition (Psychology)--Fiction. 3. English language--Spelling--Fiction.] I. Title.
PZ7,H43177Wh 1997
[Fic]--DC21   97-22159
                                        CIP
                                        AC

The short story "Bleached Wheat" was previously published in Emrys Journal in Spring 1996, Volume 13. Reprinted with permission.

White Bread Competition

ACKNOWLEDGEMENTS

Many special thanks to Luz and Justina's birth/publishing family:

Denise Chávez, the angel looking out for me; *el abuelito*, Piri Thomas, who gave me his blessings; the godmothers, Marie Brown, Lesley Anne Brown (greatest agents), Yolanda Lopez (fabulous artist) and to the godfathers Floyd Salas, Alejandro Murgía and Marcus Lopez; *a las tías*, Marcia Reese, Patti McWillams *y* Billie Letts; *a las hermanas*, Carol MacDonald, Lucy Blake-Elahi *y* Deb Trent; *a las comadres*, Stacia Tolman, Marlene Smythe, Doris House Rice, Alice Davis-Rains, Gail Williams, Lois Joy, Betsy Damon, Mary Noble, Margaret Muñez *y* Judy Serebrin; *el primo*, Seko Franklin *y la prima*, Maricela Trujillo, who supported and believed in me through it all; to the homies at the Office Depot for the zillion and one copies and the gang at the Post Office for figuring out all the postage *y a la gente* at Arte Público Press, Marina Tristán, Carole Juarez, Russell Williams and Mickey James; *a las mujeres* with attitude at the Women of Color Resource Center, Linda Burnham, Miriam Louie and Aimie Gresham; to the women at *Galeria de la Raza* for their concern and enthusiasm; *a la nieta*, Jasmine Mi Lavallee; *y los hijos*, Thanh and Jay Lavallee, they taught me much and never gave up on me; to all those who saw me when I couldn't and touched my life with their presence and their prayers, and the stand-still man with his wicked crooked grin, may he one day climb out and find me again.

TABLE OF CONTENTS

Page

White Bread Competition

My sister's big smile would be very heavy to carry home if she didn't win today.

The Auditorium at South San High School was jammed full with people waiting for the spelling bee to start. Students waved signs with the names of people competing—"Jiving with Sekou" or "Marisela Is #1." Luz, my sister, was older than me by two years, and in the ninth grade. She sat on the stage among the other kids who were all on metal folding chairs set in a row. She didn't have to wear braids. Her black hair, styled in a bob, fell just above her shoulders. Our *tías* were always touching her hair because it was so thick and always saying how beautiful it was. She didn't look at anyone else on stage; she just sat there with a big smile on her face.

My three best friends, Sofia Cuellar, Diana Ortíz, Sally Jane Mendoza and I stood up and shouted, "*¡Viva Luz!*" several times. Sofia stuck a fist in the air. Diana jiggled in her seat with excitement.

Sally Jane tugged at my skirt. "Justina, watch out." Mrs. Garza, the school monitor, hurried over to us and made us sit down, telling us we were acting like *pachucas*. Sally Jane made a face behind Mrs. Garza's back.

Across the aisle from us, Kathy, Virginia and two of their girlfriends, all from the fancy Alamo Heights area, were laughing at us as the school monitor walked away. Each held a sign with one word that, all together, read, "All the way Debbie." Debbie, Kathy's older sister, with curly blonde hair and a silk blue blouse under a plaid jumper, was sitting on the stage next to Luz.

The four of us jumped up and yelled, "*¡Viva Luz!*" as the school principal walked onto the stage. We dropped to our seats before Mrs. Garza could stand up.

The words flashed on a screen above their heads, faster than a video game character, yet each contestant spat out the correct letters. I knew how important this was for Luz. She had a straight-A report card and each correct answer got her closer to the scholarship she wanted for college.

I gripped Sally Jane's hand, my knuckles turning white. Luz had sworn me to secrecy. Our parents didn't know she was in the finals. It would be too hard to have to tell them if she lost.

Ten of the fifteen kids had misspelled. Only five stood out in front now. Luz's smile was still as bright as it had been an hour ago. My stomach burned like the inside of a volcano, as if I had eaten too many chiles. Spelling doesn't come easy to me. Nothing much about school did. Luz was the star and our whole family was proud of her. She would go far, they kept saying.

Two more people sat. The three up front stood closer together. My heart banged in my chest. I thought for sure that the girls next to me could hear it. But I didn't bother looking at them; my eyes were hooked with a telepathic beam on Luz. She had to win. She had to because she wanted to so very much. My sister would be miserable is she lost, more for all of us than even for herself.

The third person sat. Now it was only Debbie and Luz standing alone on each end of the stage. I held my breath when Luz had to spell Mississippi. On her next word, we clutched each other's hands when she correctly spelled the word M-I-S-S-P-E-L-L-E-D. We looked at each other and shrugged. It appeared that Luz was getting all the hard words. Luz could do it. I just knew she could.

As my big sister, she had always done everything first and better. I was proud of her. She was the one who was making it easier for me. She would be the first to do it all. I had no doubts. When she spelled the next word right, I stuck my fist into the air. She was a winner, no matter what happened next, and she was my sister!

Then Debbie missed. We mouthed prayers to Our Lady of Guadalupe as Luz slowly spelled F-U-C-H-S-I-A. Our fingers ached as we seized each other's hand, but we didn't care.

My mouth was dry as the next word flashed on the screen. I sucked in my cheeks. I looked at Sofia, who was the smartest one of us, and she shrugged. She didn't know the word. How would Luz?

Luz was silent for what felt like a thousand years. Then she smiled a face-cracking smile and spelled C-H-R-Y-S-A-N-T-H-E-M-U-M. We were on our feet. Everyone, brown, black, red, and yellow, was yelling and cheering. Luz had won!

———

Usually I ate lunch outside with the other girls who had bean *taquitos* just like mine. But this time my friends wanted to be included with the older students. No one noticed the pesky little sister in the way.

Mis amigas and I were on one side of the lunch room table. Sofia, tiny, five feet, flushed with excitement, her dark skin crimson, sat next to me. She brushed her long black hair off one shoulder. Taller by three inches and several pounds heavier, Diana, whose brown hair was held back by pink butterfly barrettes, sat next to her.

Sally Jane sat at the end. She had light brown hair and light skin and a *mamá* who made sure that everyone knew her grandparents had come from Spain. We didn't care, except when Sally Jane would forget she was the same brown as we were. The three of us would ignore her for a little while and soon the white girls would remind Sally Jane that they never forgot she was mostly *Mexicana*.

My sister, her best friend, Arturo, and two other Chicanas from her class sat opposite us. I took bites from my tortilla, hidden underneath the wax paper.

Debbie and her girlfriends stopped at our table. Even her little sister Kathy trailed behind them. They waved hands wearing rings that were forbidden by school policy.

"Congratulations, Luz," said Debbie. "But don't think you're going to represent San Antonio at the National. This was only the first round. Don't get too comfortable."

Arturo took a big bite from his sandwich and said, "Yeah—you should know, runner-up!"

Everyone laughed, including me. Kathy nudged Debbie and pointed at me. They sniffed.

"What's that I smell?" She stretched out her arm. I saw the finger coming my way and felt scared. I didn't know what she wanted from me.

With the tip of her finger, she lifted the wax paper off my taco. "You're eating peanut butter on a tortilla! How gross!" Debbie cried for everyone to hear.

I looked into Kathy's blue eyes as she said, "You're in America now. Why don't you eat American food?"

Arturo jumped to his feet. Several boys, who were sitting across the aisle, sprang to their feet.

The cafeteria monitor bounced out of his chair and headed in our direction.

Debbie took Kathy by the arm.

"C'mon, Kathy. You know, you can take them out of the field, but you can't take the field out of them." The four girls, my two classmates, and all the students eating lunch laughed. Everyone except us at our table.

I hung my head.

My sister hissed at me from across the table. "Keep your head up high, Justina."

I did as she told me. "I'm sorry to ruin your happy day," I said.

"Eat your taco with pride."

I stared at her, trying to see if some monster from outer space had taken over her body. My bossy sister was telling me to eat this tortilla with pride? Just yesterday she made me walk with her down the hallway to throw away the plastic wrapper with "Tortillas made in San Antonio" written across the front that *abuelita* had used to bag the tacos. Now she was telling me to eat my food with pride just because some white girls made fun of me.

I was about to say something back to her when another burst of loud laughter came from the table across the aisle. I swallowed my anger at my sister, crumpled the paper with the taco inside it, and tossed the heap onto the pile of trash on the cafeteria tray.

On the way home from school, *mis amigas* were talking about what they were going to wear when they went to see Luz win. They had no doubts. She would be the first Chicana to win and they wanted to look fine.

The sidewalk heated the bottom of my shoes. I walked, watching my feet drag alongside the others. My satchel hung from my hand; the strap scraped the concrete. Sweat stung my eyes, but I didn't wipe it away because I didn't want anyone to think I was crying. I had disappointed my sister. Those girls had laughed at us because of what I didn't have. I had taken my sister's great moment and messed it up. She had avoided me after school and I didn't blame her. I wished I could avoid me, too.

The others kept me inside their chatter, ignoring that I wasn't saying much. A woman with a bag of groceries in her arms walked around as we turned a corner.

"Justina, where are you?" whined Sally Jane.

"You better catch up with us, or else you know what could happen." Diana touched the pink barrette in her hair to make sure she hadn't lost it.

I walked backwards to where they were and spun around. "Did you notice what was sticking out of the top of her bag?" They shook their heads. Sally Jane twisted her neck around the corner to see.

"Let's go." I walked past them and they followed, complaining. I walked through the double glass doors of the H.E.B.

Diana shuddered and wrapped her arms around herself. "Hijo, this grocery store is freezing."

"Let's go," I said, and headed down the aisle.

"What for?" asked Sofia, pulling Diana by the arm to stay even with Sally Jane and me.

"I know," said Sally Jane, swinging her knapsack around her legs.

I threw a dare over my shoulder. "So what?"

"So what—what?" Sofia twisted her head from me to Sally Jane, walking fast to keep up.

I stopped in front of the bread rack. The others crashed behind me.

Sally Jane smirked. "She gonna buy white bread so she can eat sandwiches for lunch."

"What of it?" I glared at Sally Jane, making her take a step back.

Her smirk vanished and she shrugged. "Just making an observation."

"Right. Go observe somewhere else. I don't need your grief right now."

Sally Jane raised her hands in surrender. "Fine with me."

"Fine with me, too." We stared for several moments before Sally Jane looked away. I turned and faced the bread rack.

I felt as if I had opened the book to the math quiz and all the problems with all the angles were there in front of me. "So many kinds."

Sally Jane said in a voice that sounded a lot like our teacher, "Oh yeah. We've tried this kind and this one, too. They were too cheap." With her chin, she pointed at the row of bread above our heads. "That's the kind we eat. It's way too expensive for you."

"Oh-oh." Diana covered her mouth, waiting for the fireworks.

"You think you're such hot stuff. You think no one is as good as you." I moved toward her, my hands growing into fists.

Sofia stepped between us. "You know she's stupid with that light-skin-better-than stuff. Don't let her get to you." With a jerk of her head, she urged me on.

Sally Jane pretended all innocence. "Ay, I was just telling you what kind we..."

Sofia wheeled on her and scowled. "This is what Justina wants to do. Shut up."

Sally Jane stuck her hands out in front of her. "Fine with me. I was just trying to be helpful."

Diana, standing behind her, said, "Well, don't. We don't need it. Justina knows what she's doing."

"This is the one I'm gonna buy," I said and picked the one Sally Jane had pointed to. Snubbing her as I walked by, I headed for the check-out with Diana and Sofia on my heels and Sally Jane trailing behind.

My grandmother stood at the stove, stirring a pot of frijoles. She laid the spoon down and went back to the kitchen counter. She was making *tortillas* for my father's supper when he returned home from delivering mail. The skin on her hands looked like a crushed brown paper bag, yet her hands were strong as she kneaded the *masa*. Her hair hung down her back in a braid streaked with gray. She wore a black, felt reservation hat with the beaded hatband. A brown *cigarillo* hung from her lips. She would smoke it after supper.

My mother sat in her white uniform, drinking coffee at the table, talking with her mother, ready to work all night at the hospital. I proudly placed the loaf of bread on the table. My mother stared at it. Her face, the color of warm molasses, wrinkled up in confusion as she asked, "What is this?" Her hair, soft and curly, swung freely around her neck. Her fingernails, spotted with different colors of paint, were the clues that she had been painting today.

"Butter Krust loaf of white bread."

"I know what it is, but what is it?"

"Butter Krust..."

"Who bought it?"

"I did." I clicked my heels together, and if they hadn't been sneakers, I know they would have made noise.

"Honey, you spent your allowance on this bread?"

I nodded as I corrected, "White bread."

Abuelita turned from the stove, took the cigar from her mouth, and stared at the loaf. She snorted. "I could have made a bigger one than that." She twisted back to the stove and flipped the tortilla on the grill, putting the cigar in its familiar groove with the other hand. My mother leaned over so her face was even with mine. "*Mijita, ¿por qué?*"

"I want to take sandwiches for lunch." My sureness was spilling from my heels at the look on my mother's face.

The screen door slammed behind my sister as she ran into the kitchen yelling, "Hey, everyone, guess what happened?" She sneaker-squeaked to a stop in front of the table and spotted the loaf. "White bread. All right!" She looked at our mother. "Sandwiches for lunch?"

My mother shrugged. "You will have to ask your sister. She bought it."

Luz faced me. "Oh."

My mother watched the silent exchange.

"So, can I?" Luz asked again.

"Sure, because you won the spelling bee today," I said.

My mother clapped her hands. "*Mijita*, how great it is! Let's celebrate."

I grinned and nodded eagerly, looking forward to having all the relatives over to the house. We were all so proud of Luz.

With both hands, I carried the loaf of bread to the far end of the counter so no one would squash it. I wanted perfect sandwiches for school tomorrow.

Off the kitchen counter, mi *abuelita* grabbed her black reservation hat and with a flick of her wrist, she tossed it on top of the bread. No one dared touch her flat-brimmed hat. My bread was safe. I smiled at my grandmother.

The next morning, we woke late. Mamá hurried us out the door, but I stalled to check my lunch bag. At the bottom of the bag sat the white bread sandwich, wrapped in wax paper. I gave my mother a squeeze around her waist and ran to join mis amigas.

At our lockers, I announced to my girlfriends that I was eating lunch in the cafeteria.

"But why? It's fresher outside." Sofia slammed her locker door.

"Fresh air and fresh boys." Diana grinned, clicking her locker door shut. Today she wore blue turtle barrettes.

"I know why she wants to eat in the cafeteria." Sally Jane's ponytail danced.

Sofia and Diana watched; Sofia bit her lip, and Diana twirled her finger around her hair.

Sally Jane pointed at my lunch bag with her elbow. "She brought a sandwich in her lunch."

"Really?" Sofia and Diana responded, their eyes growing as big as pesos.

"You do what you want. I'm eating in the cafeteria." I spun away. I knew they would follow me. I knew they would stick by me, as we had always done for each other. At least, I was hoping really hard that they would, so I wouldn't be alone.

In the cafeteria, my sister, sitting with her friends a table row away, didn't wave back to me, but then she never did when she was with her friends. I spotted Debbie and her girlfriends in line for hot food. I sat at the table, near where they usually sat, waiting for them to pass by.

A few minutes later, Sofia and Diana sat across from me. Sally Jane sat next to me. We smiled at each other. Sofia reported the latest romantic troubles of the beautiful women and men in the *novelas* on TV. She was the only one whose mother allowed her to watch the *novelas*, especially "*Simplemente María*." She kept us all up-to-date on what they wore and who loved whom and especially who was "living in sin."

Debbie, her girlfriends, and her sister Kathy wore stud earrings, hair ribbons, and faces masked with enough make-up to be against the school rules. They cornered the last table and walked down the aisle. I

popped open my lunch bag and pulled out my sandwich. I flattened the brown paper bag with one hand
and set my prize on top. I carefully unfolded the wax
paper, spreading each piece flat against the table. The
sandwich blossomed before me. It glowed white and
was spongy like *masa*.

Debbie and the others were setting their trays
down next to the boys from eight grade, when Kathy
glanced over at our table and spotted my sandwich.
She nudged Debbie.

I wrapped both hands around the sandwich. Loud
laughing and hollering filled the room. Everyone at
the table where my sister sat was poking each other
and acting funny. My sister sat in the middle of all
that noise, quiet and small.

Sally Jane stood up and stretched her neck to see
what was happening.

I lifted the sandwich for my first big bite when the
laughter jumped across the room.

I looked at Debbie and Kathy giggling, their shoulders butting each other in rhythm. I heard Sally Jane
say, "Oh, oh."

I turned back to my first white bread sandwich
and opened my mouth. I felt like this was the last
breath of air I would ever want to take.

The bean broth had soaked the bottom slice of
bread and turned it brown. The pressure from my
hands ripped the soggy bread. The frijoles were dropping out from the side of the bread and landing on
top of the wax paper like brown freckles. My hands

dripped with juice and sliding frijoles. *Mi abuelita* had made us bean sandwiches.

⟡

When I arrived home, I opened the door and ran to my bedroom. My mother cried out, *"Hola"* from the living room, but I didn't answer and shut my bedroom door very quietly. I didn't want my mother coming in to ask me a bunch of questions that I didn't have answers for.

I lay on my bed and watched the skies turn a bruised blue through the window. I didn't change my clothes; I didn't cry. I listened to all the noises that made up my family: the baby laughing as my sister fed him, my father and brother wrestling. My father spoke in a voice that tumbled into my room like thunder from the top of a mountain. My brother answered in a voice that reached for the same heights but only screeched in places.

I wondered why I was so different. Why couldn't I want what everyone else in my family wanted, to be happy with the things that were here? Why did it matter what anyone else thought?

A long arm of light cut across my bed when my mother opened the door. "Justina, are you feeling well?"

I nodded, afraid for her to hear the pain in my voice.

"Mijita."

"I just want to be alone," I pushed the words out hard, too hard. My *mamá's* face was the same color as my dark room. Her brown eyes were soft with sympathy. Her black hair curved under and bounced off the collar of her white hospital uniform; her thin artist hands reached out to me.

She sat on the edge of the bed and stroked my arm. "I've talked to your sister."

I jumped into my mother's waiting arms and cried. She rubbed my back and rocked the pain from my body.

"I just wanted to be something nice like them." I sobbed between the words.

"*Mijita*, you have to be strong. You can't let them get you down. We think you're very special."

"You're my mother. You're supposed to say that."

My mother pushed me back from her, smiling. "*Mijita*, I can tell you what I believe. It's up to you to decide how beautiful you are."

"But, but..."

"*¿Qué?*"

I couldn't tell her that I was ashamed of my color. She would hate me forever. "But the teachers say..."

My mother's voice gained an edge to it. "Are you going to let the ignorance of others tell you what's real about your own life?"

"But they're the teachers. They know everything."

"Let me tell you something, *mijita*..."

"You just don't understand, Mom. It's a lot different from when you were little. Lots different."

I pushed away from the warmth of her arms, got off the bed, and changed into my nightgown. She watched me for a little while; the space between her eyebrows pinched tight from thinking hard. But there was nothing she could tell me that I didn't know already.

Two days later, during third period, the teacher announced, "Children, put your pencils and books away. Today we have a special treat."

The buzz of questions skated across the room as we packed our books.

"Today we have a guest speaker. She has volunteered to speak to us about something very important. It is about the food we eat. Say hello to Mrs. Rosaura Ríos."

I slipped down in my seat, trying hard to become invisible. Sally Jane and Sofia looked at me. I shrugged. I hadn't known she was coming. Diana waved at my mother with a big smile on her face.

The whole class rang out, "Hello, Mrs. Ríos." Several boys, who sat in a bunch in the back, snorted. One called out, "Beaner."

Mrs. Letts stepped to the front of the room and clapped her hands. "Silence."

She stared her Darth Vadar stare—her face didn't move a muscle, her eyes didn't blink, her jaw thrust forward—until everyone quieted down.

"Mrs. Ríos was gracious enough to come in to make this presentation. We owe her the courtesy of giving her our complete attention and our most respectful behavior." She waited a moment, the weight of her gaze silencing each student.

"Good. Mrs. Ríos, the class is yours." The blonde teacher stretched her hand out, palm up, offering my mother the room.

I was thankful that she had on a red-and-yellow-flowered dress instead of the janitor's white uniform; it made her look pretty and her skin richer, darker like cinnamon. I felt a mixture of pride and total embarrassment.

"Today I want to tell you a story that began before there were any people from Europe living in this country. Thousands of years ago, there was a tribe of people called the Aztecs that lived in a place we now call Mexico."

I saw Kathy, Debbie's little sister, look at Virginia and roll her eyes. I moved so that I was hidden behind the person in front of me.

"There was much hunger. People and their children didn't have enough to eat. There was much suffering in all the villages.

"One day, a woman was walking through the woods searching for something to feed her family. She discovered a trail of ants, coming out of their home and traveling up into the mountain.

"She hid to watch these ants because she knew they were very hard workers." My mother crunched her shoulders forward as if she were hiding, and I covered my eyes with my hand.

"Soon she discovered that they were coming back carrying blue corn. She asked the ants to show her where the blue corn was hidden because her family was very hungry. But the ants would not tell her their secret. She went home very, very tired." She leaned against the teacher's desk and wiped her brow. I wanted the floor to open and swallow me whole.

My mother perked up and raised a finger into the air. "Her youngest children were twin boys who became very sad when they saw their mother crying. So they took off during the night and climbed up to the moon and asked the moon to help their mother. *La Luna* sent her beams down to the earth. The waters roared and tumbled all night, but the mountain did not give up any of its treasures.

"Morning came and the twins asked the sun if he would help their mother. *El Sol* made angry clouds at the ants for being so selfish. There was a great storm with giant bolts of lightning. The sun sent one huge bolt of lightning which split the mountain in two. All the blue corn inside spilled out and the village people rushed to fill their baskets."

Once again my mother slouched into her disappointed position. A couple of boys in the back of the room snickered. The teacher, standing behind my mother, shook her head at them.

"The sun was very disappointed in the ants and sent another bolt of lightning which turned the ants red. They were so hot to touch; no one want anything to do with them. There was such a cry from all the ants. The lightning was the hottest the sun had ever made, so hot that it turned all the corn yellow. And that is how we know the corn today."

Her hands moved in circles in front of her like propellers. "Everyone was very happy for a long time.

Then some men from across the ocean came upon our land. They were pale and weak from their trip. When they saw the fields of yellow corn growing, they thought they had found the land of gold." She arched her hands over her head.

"They had a little of the white bread they had brought from their home, but it was green with mold and was making everyone sick. They were all about to die, when the King of the tribe invited them to eat with him."

At this point, my mother stood taller, more proud. "At the King's table, he had a kind of bread the men from across the ocean had never seen. It was flat, but stronger than their white bread. It could hold more food to keep them from hunger as they traveled. They asked the king what was this food. He told them it was a tortilla."

Here my mother lowered her voice with doom. "These men took our homes, broke up our villages, and even killed many of us, but they never could take away our language and our food.

"To this day, the food we eat is the same food that kept those men from across the ocean alive. It is the same food that the priest would offer up to the Gods in the heavens, the same food that was served to the Aztec kings of many years ago."

My mother stood up straight, her hands slowly coming to rest, one cupped in the other, at her waist. "The food of the Chicanos is not just everyday food. It's food that has come down many generations. Our food is our history."

No one made a sound when my mother finished. My teacher thanked her and then asked if anyone had questions. The boys that had giggled at her before asked, "The twin sons? Did they know any karate?"

My mother smiled. "Probably. But they didn't need it because they could climb up to the stars to talk with the moon and the sun, so who would bother them?"

His friend punched him on his arm. The Chicano students sat taller in their seats.

My stomach flipped as if I were on a roller coaster when Kathy raised her hand. She smiled as she stood. "Isn't it true that that kind of food is really only for poor people?"

My mother smiled and I thought, oh, oh. I knew that smile well. "Do you and your parents ever eat out?"

Kathy threw a look at Virginia, then answered, "Of course."

The smile never changed and I knew the machete was coming fast. "Where was the last place you ate out?"

Without hesitation, Kathy answered, "*La Hacienda.*"

The smile disappeared. She stood with her head arched out. "People pay lots of money to eat our poor simple food that kings ate." She winked to Diana who smiled brightly in return.

Kathy opened her mouth, but the teacher quieted her with a pointed finger. A boy in back stood up and asked, "What kind of weapons did they have in those days? Any Uzis?" The teacher sat him down with another finger-pointing gesture and ended the question period. She shook my mother's hand and had the whole class say "thank you" aloud.

I felt so much relief that my mother didn't talk to me in the classroom before she left.

After class at our lockers, Sofia and Diana were taking their lunches out of their lockers. Sally Jane looked around me. I heard Kathy's group coming up behind me.

"That story was so quaint," said Kathy. "It actually brought tears to my eyes." The rest of the girls in her group giggled.

Another girl cut into the laughter. "Didn't she talk funny? Her accent was so cute?" She pushed her thick glasses up her nose with her middle finger.

I balled my hands in fists with a look filled of threat and menace. Sally Jane edged beside me, fists in the air. Swinging her waist-length black hair over her shoulder, Sofia, all five feet of her, dropped her books and spit out, "You *chupa*. We were here before you." Diana hoisted me back by the arm, halting our forward motion as a teacher strolled by, smiling at us all.

As the teacher rounded the corner, Kathy shoved Sally Jane as she walked by.

Sally Jane bounced off the locker and the three of us stepped in front of Sally Jane to keep her from tackling Kathy.

Virginia stepped out of the gang of girls as the group moved on.

"I thought the story was, you know, really great." She hugged her books to her chest.

Diana sneered. "Who cares?"

Kathy looked back. "Ginny, catch up." She reeled Virginia back into the group with a smile that had sharp teeth in it. "What did you say to them? Something really good?"

"Yeah. Of course." Virginia looked back and blinked both eyes.

Sally Jane muttered curses.

Sofia shook her head. "Now you gonna have to go to confession."

Diana nodded. "For having bad thoughts."

Sally Jane smiled. "Nah. These are really good thoughts."

We all laughed.

"Let's go eat in there." I moved ahead of them toward the cafeteria.

Diana looked at me as if I had frijoles stuck in my hair. "Justina, are you bonkers?" She and Sofia got on either side of me.

Sally Jane said, "You looking for trouble? Because I'm ready."

Sofia and Diana nodded at Sally Jane's invitation.

"Nah. No trouble."

"Then what?" persisted Sally Jane as she followed me toward the cafeteria.

"My mom. It took a lot of guts today. If she can do that, I can go in there."

Sally Jane grinned. "Let's do it."

Sofia nodded. "We have as much right to be in there as they do."

Diana didn't say anything; she just opened the door for us.

Kathy and Virginia purposely sat across the aisle from us. We had ignored them throughout the lunch period.

We had finished and were pushing the chairs back under the table when Kathy, sitting second from the end, sang out, "Did you enjoy your sandwich?"

Sally Jane said, "Leave Justina alone." Her light brown hair jigged in a ponytail.

Kathy scoffed, "Can't she talk for herself?"

Sally Jane advanced another step toward their table. "If she did, you'd be sorry."

Kathy touched the arm of the boy sitting next to her. "Oh, I'm so scared," she said, waving her hand in front of her face. "Maybe you all should just stick to where you belong."

Sally Jane stepped up to the table, picked up a milk container, leaned over the guy, and poured it down the front of Kathy's peach silk blouse.

Kathy sat with her mouth opened wide and her arms outstretched as her eyes tracked the descent of the milk falling through the air. Her shoulders turned inward with the shock of the cold milk as it splashed down the front of her new blouse. The two boys sitting on either side of her twisted away to avoid the splashing milk.

Screeching, Kathy shoved her tray forward, bumping it into Virginia's tray across the table. The bowl on Virginia's tray slid across the slick surface and toppled over the edge, splashing soup onto her lap. Virginia bounced to her feet, hollering, "It's hot!" She sobbed loudly as girls on both sides of her dabbed napkins against her legs and picked the noodles off.

Pulling her blouse away from her body, Kathy stared at Sally Jane, eyes sending torturous messages. "My mother will make sure you are never permitted back into school."

The two boys at the end of the table rose and stood like sentries in the aisle, towering over Sally Jane. Sofia and Diana skirted around Sally Jane and took their place on each side of her. Their eyes glared machete messages at the two boys.

Sofia, barely reaching the mid-section of the boy in front of her, held her fist in the air, swinging her black hair over her shoulder. Diana flipped her middle finger at the other boy. Having grown-up with five older brothers, she had no doubts about taking him down.

Boys and girls from surrounding tables were on their feet, hollering and yelling. Kathy whipped up her dish of vanilla pudding and swung her arm back to throw it as the cafeteria monitor grabbed Sally Jane by the arm and pulled her out of range.

While everyone cheered for Sally Jane as the monitor dragged her out of the cafeteria, I stepped across the aisle. Swinging my arm, I hooked Kathy's hand that still held the dish of vanilla pudding and it crashed on the floor.

Sofia cheered, "*¡Andale!*" Diana grinned.

"*Las Amigas*" walked out of the cafeteria with our heads high.

Too Many Cooks

The *vaquero's* silver guns, his black suit, and his curly, black paper mustache jerked violently up and down. Controlling the rope, *Tío* Hector pulled hard to keep the piñata out of range of the child slashing the air with a sawed-off broom handle wrapped in blue and pink crepe paper. A dozen children stood ready to pounce when the child with the broom handle split the piñata, showering the goodies into their waiting hands. Luz was cutting across the yard to be with her girlfriends when she stopped to watch the vaquero sway in the breeze.

Like an old-time vaudeville hook, an arm around her neck drew her into a group standing near the rosebush. Wait till *Mamá* sees the empty bottles under the roses. She will be so angry. Her *Tío* Ambrose twisted her around to face her aunt.

"This girl here is going to prove to the world that all Mexican-Americans are not like what they see in the movies."

Tío Ambrose's wife pinched Luz's cheeks and stroked the girl's black shoulder-length hair into shape. *Tía* Gloria eyed the telltale signs of the woman blooming within; the thickening of lips, the drape of her long lashes over her brown eyes. "We are so proud of you, Luz."

"Making it to the city spelling contest. Before we know it, we'll be in Austin, going to the state capital to see you win there." She leaned forward on her crutches, her shoulders hunched toward her ears as she supported herself. The hem of her long skirt fluttered with her movement. She had lost her left leg from below the knee to diabetes after she had had her son.

"Thank you, *Tía* Gloria." *¡Híjole!* What do I do? She looks like she's gonna fall any second. Major embarrassment if she falls on me.

"She knows she had an obligation and a duty to our kind. We help each other out." *Tía* Gloria dimmed the lights around her with her smile.

Here we go again with that "our kind" stuff. How am I supposed to know where I belong?

Tío Ambrose frowned as he plopped an arm over his niece's shoulders. "I've talked with your father and I told him, this is no thing a girl should be doing. Too dangerous. You are so young. Such a rose." He pointed at her with the hand that was holding the beer bottle.

Just before the party, he was telling me I was clumsy.

Tía Gloria blurted, "It's men like you with attitudes like we're such a rose that forces us women to be strong." Ambrose stiffened. *Tía* Gloria glared at her husband like a matador watching the bull kick up the dirt.

"*Tío* Ambrose I'll be all right."

Phew! His breath reeked. I wonder who will fall down first—*mi tía* or *mi tío?*

She adjusted the weight of her uncle's arm over her shoulder, smiling politely at her *tío's* friends. Her uncle was an older replica of her father; thin, brown, weathered, with calloused hands and knotted knuckles.

Mr. Rosales grinned, "With those dark eyes, this little one can get my help anytime."

Ay! It's time to get out of here. Got to warn my girlfriends—"Roman Hands" Rosales is on the make.

Her aunt slapped her husband's arm and jerked her head in Rosales's direction. Her uncle halted his friend with a raised hand. "Cuidado. Es mi sobrina."

The short man shrugged. "For a squirt, she is the prettiest one in the family."

Her uncle nudged her in the direction she had been heading.

San Antonio's seaty afternoon had cooled into a sweet, flower-smelling night. Throughout the backyard, mesquite-flavored smoke from the huge grill hovered over the heads of the people at the party. Everyone knows smoke follows the pretty girls.

Men in plaid and light-colored, short-sleeved shirts stood in groups, some with one foot on a folding chair, all waving arms, arguing into each others' sentences, holding plastic tumblers filled with foam-topped brew. *Ay Díos mío*, how do they know what they are saying? No one listens to the other.

Women, in dresses of bright-colored flowers or ice cream stripes, sat on lawn chairs huddled in groups of two or three, exchanging news of their childrens' accomplishments or judging the flirting abilities of the younger women. Listening to them, you'd believe that all their children were going to be doctors and lawyers.

The young women pretended to ignore the stares from the young men that they had seduced into noticing them. Young men envied the freedom of the small children as they divulged, with heads bent together, loud and with authority, their conquests, their chests growing bigger with every assertion. Ay, don't they ever get tired of hearing their own voices.

Small children wrestled on the ground, grass staining the boy's white Sunday-best shirts their mothers had ironed the day before. Girls ran with untied ribbons flying after their pretty flowered dresses. Boys practiced the cock walk—chest out, hips swinging—of their older brothers. Girls were caught between the urges to punch a boy's face or kiss it. Just another family gathering.

"Here you are. I was looking for you." Luz stopped on her tiptoes to avoid bumping into her mother. Hijo, here goes the party. Mrs. Ríos's hands were loaded with several plates topped with silverware, napkins and paper cups. She pushed the load off toward Luz's middle. Luz quickly lifted her arms to catch the utensils. She swayed and took a step backwards with the sudden weight.

Oh, man, I just want to go hang with my girl-friends.

"Here. Take these to your *abuelita's* table. I don't want her coming into the kitchen." Her mother, a head taller than Luz with the same brown eyes and thick black hair, wiped her forehead and tucked a strand of hair behind her ear in one sweep of her hand. She cast her gaze across the backyard, checking each group of relatives and friends. All appeared well taken care of. With a shove to her daughter's shoulder, she hustled Luz on her way. "Get going before your *abuelita* gets nosy."

I'm always the one that has to do everything. She never asks my sister to do anything.

Luz looked with envy at her girlfriends. Colored lights hung from poles hooked on the fence; blue and white crepe paper, twisted together, dropped across the fence in the rear of the yard. In front of the garage stood a long table with a stereo on one end. The eight-year-old birthday boy eyed the brightly wrapped birthday gifts on the other end. There, her girlfriends huddled under a string of pink flamingos that glowed brightly. They were pretending not to notice the young men who were pretending not to notice them. The driveway was swept clean for dancing. Her girlfriends were choosing cassettes for the tape player that would entice the young men to move from their corner at the end of the driveway. They're having all the fun. I want to be over there with them.

Luz's girlfriends were motioning for her to join them. She raised the plates in her hands in the direction of her grandmother's table as an explanation to them. Giggling, they turned back to the selection of the next tune, except for Ana and Olga.

Luz, still walking, caught Ana noticing a slight head movement from one of the young machos. Ana probably thinks Ricardo wants to be with her. Olga is nodding like she thinks he means it for her. Flirt all you want. He belongs to me, brujas! Luz sighed as she reached her grandmother's table.

"*Abuelita*, let me set the table for you," Luz said as she nodded respectfully at the three elderly women gathered around the table.

"*Mijita*, que linda. You are such a good help." *Abuelita* looked at the two women on her left and nodded with pride. The cross-stitch of wrinkles across her face blurred in the smoke of her thin, brown cigarillo. "You will make a good wife soon." Her black, felt reservation hat with the beaded hatband sat on the back of her head.

Oh, no, not more talk about getting married. Will she ever get off that kick? Luz almost tossed the dishes in front of each woman.

"This business of the spelling wasp." Her grandmother leaned forward.

"Spelling bee," Luz said with a deep sigh. Her grandmother was so ancient; she didn't know anything.

"Sí, el insecto."

Luz sighed again, louder. She never gets it, no matter how often I tell her. ¡Qué triste!

"This is not to bother with. You are of the age to think hard of marriage."

Right! Over my dead brain.

Mrs. Fuentes, who was Olga's grandmother, asked, "How old she is?" She had to lean forward in the chair because her feet didn't touch the ground.

"Fourteen just last month," replied Luz. The heck with the silverware. I gotta get out of here before they marry me off.

Mrs. Fuentes' chins swayed. "My oldest was already born when I got to be sixteen."

It's going to be different for me.

Mrs. Tijerina, Ana's grandmother, said, "You have a husband picked out from them." She pointed with a shift of her eyes to the group of young men playing horseshoes beside the garage.

Luz rolled her eyes as one boy squirted another with a shaken-up soda. Oh, puhleeeze! "*Abuelita*, you know I'm going to college. The money I win at the spelling contest will help me get there."

The tip of the *cigarillo* reddened as Aura sucked in air. "It's that mother of yours." Luz's grandmother pulled her flat-brimmed hat low on her forehead, hiding her eyes.

Ay, I blew it. Time to hit the road.

"This thing with the college gets our kind nothing. It takes our children and turns them against us." The ash from the *cigarillo* fell onto the table and burned a hole in the red-and-white-checkered, plastic table-cloth. "This is not good."

Mrs. Fuentes nodded, leaned back, her feet swinging in midair, and folded her arms in righteousness.

Mrs. Tijerina nodded and ran her fingers over the rosary she always carried in her pocket. She checked to make sure that Ana was still within sight.

Looks like time for the human sacrifice. This here virgin is on her way. The three elderly women glared disapproval as Luz walked away backwards.

Before she took five steps, Mrs. Cuellar captured her by the arm. Her black curls bobbed along the sides of her head.

Ay, she's so beautiful. Her face is like the magazine models, painted and smooth.

"Luz, your *mamá* must be so happy with you." Mrs. Cuellar, pretty in a tight, blue-flowered, red dress, patted Luz's hand.

Mrs. Cuellar had taken as many beers as Mr. Cuellar from the shed next to the back door. A huge metal washtub, full of ice, sat on top of the dryer in the shed, keeping the beer cold. Something always happens when these two have had one too many.

Mrs. Cuellar shoved Luz in front of Mrs. Ortíz. "You showed all those gringos at school that we Chicanas have brains. Brains and guts." Mrs. Cuellar used her little finger to wipe off a smidgen of deep plum lipstick from the corner of her mouth.

Mrs. Ortíz put one hand on Luz's right shoulder. Luz stared at Mrs. Ortíz's neck that was a different color than her face, the thick make-up ending at the jaw line. Mrs. Ortíz, with lips the same plum as Mrs. Cuellar, jabbed the air with the long metal serving spoon in her other hand. "Don't let no one tell you you can't be smart just because you're a girl."

That's dumb. They say I'm not smart because I'm Chicana.

Mrs. Cuellar and Mrs. Ortíz traded looks loaded with accusations and experiences.

"We need more women like you in the revolution. We have been oppressed for so long that we have to rise up and get stronger." Mrs. Cuellar poked her face so close that Luz felt her eyes cross. "Men think they can do it by themselves. But it's us women who do all the hard work. Women are stronger because we have to do more, put up with more."

All I want is for Ricardo to take me to the Social Club dance next Sunday.

Mrs. Ortíz patted Mrs. Cuellar on her shoulder in agreement. "If it wasn't for us there'd be no revolution."

"We're the ones that give birth to the warriors." Mrs. Cuellar shot a fist into the air over her head. "Yes!"

Don't let my *abuelita* hear you. She wants me married first before I even say the word "babies."

Mrs Ortíz muttered, "Right on," then they clinked their long-necked bottles.

Luz caught a signal from across the yard. She mumbled, "Excuse me," and hurried toward her mother.

Her mother shook Luz by the arm. "Go be with your girlfriends and don't be getting those two all stirred up. I love them dearly, but I'm in no mood for a revolution tonight."

Luz opened her mouth to protest, but tripped over her feet when she was shoved toward her girlfriends. I get blamed for everything. It's so unfair.

As she reached the table, Olga handed her a cup of punch. "That was close." She blinked her thick lashes that accented her green eyes.

Ana nodded, eager for gossip. "What was it about?" Ana's brown hair matched the brown of her skin and the brown of her eyes. She was all of one color. She looked beautiful and spooky all at once.

Luz shrugged. "They were talking about the spelling contest."

Olga picked up several cassettes and pretended to read the song titles. "So what? You're not gonna do it," she said casually with a shake of her head.

"I've worked hard for this. I'm going and I'm gonna win." Luz looked at the faces around her. They don't believe me. "Big time win!"

"Luz, you gone crazy?" Olga arched her trimmed and colored brows.

"You're serious about showing up?" Ana slouched against the table. Her long dangling earrings reflected light as she turned her head; her curled hair bounced with each moment.

Hijo, they're both so fancy. My father won't even let me wear stud earrings.

"You got somebody else that can do it better than me?" Luz fingered her hair.

Ana waved her hands around, flashing her different colored fingernails. "What if you lose? The whole school will be laughing at you. How embarrassing."

You should know since everyone at school laughs at you.

Licking her lips, which were glossed mocha, Olga put down the cassettes. "You know Ricardo?"

Not like I'm gonna get to know him. Luz sipped from her drink. "You have to be blind, deaf and mute not to know how Ricardo is."

Olga looked out from the side, her face hidden by a curtain of black hair. "I heard that he told this other guy that he was thinking of taking you to the Social Club dance." *¡Andale!* "But if you won, he wouldn't be want to be seen with anyone that's too brainy." She's crazy. He's taking me. He told me so.

Ana flanked her. "And if you lose, he doesn't want to hang with a loser." She pointed with the fingernail that had a rhinestone stud in it.

¡Híjolé! Luz looked from Olga to Ana, then at the faces of the rest of the girls. "So what you want me to do?" Hands on hips, feet spread apart, Luz asked, "What are you getting at?"

"Don't go," Olga said and Ana agreed.

Órale, they got together and are wearing their bright green knit dresses. Olga's hangs and flaps around her body with every breeze; Ana's rolls like a range of mountains across her torso. My mother forced me to wear this yellow dress with a sailor collar.

She said with sudden anger in her voice, "Didn't you both try out for the contest?" then she pointed at Ana, "Didn't you make it to the semifinals with me?"

"*Ay*, I missed on purpose." Sure you did. "I went far enough to show them I was smart, but not too far to get any of them mad at me." And placed her hands on her waist.

Keep squeezing it all you want, Ana. You're not going to make it any smaller than it is.

Luz's dark eyes shrunk to black pinpricks when she asked, "Mad at you for what?" Like we all know who "them" is.

"You know the white girls think they have it all bundled up."

Olga slipped in, her green eyes greener from the shine of her dress. "And guess who invited her to the dance while you're at the competition next weekend?"

Ana moved to the table behind Olga.

"Is this what you call being a friend?" Luz took a step toward Ana, clenching her hands into fists. "If you go, I'll make sure you got no hair to fix up for the thing." Or something.

Taking a step back, Ana said, "*¡Órale!* I couldn't say no." She twisted her finger in the curls of her permed hair, entangling her fingernail stud.

"See, like I told you." Olga stepped between them. "If you get too smart, the boys won't like you."

Luz heard her name called. *Tía* Gloria motioned to her that she needed another drink. We'll see who's too smart. Placing the cup on the table next to the tape deck, she tipped it over, then headed toward the punch bowl, leaving squeals of horror behind as the stain on Ana's dress spread.

A few steps from the table, she was clotheslined by Mr. Cuellar, who wasn't much taller than Luz, but had arms of solid muscles. "Here she is."

Bad news. I've seen Mr. Cuellar make more trips than anyone else to visit the tub in the shed, except his best friend. Mr. Torres keeps filling his glass with ice. He's keeping cool what he pours from the brown paper bag that he keeps in the car.

Luz had heard her mother fret over their drinking. Her father had promised her mother that he would watch over them. But he was busy at the grill, flipping meat, talking to the men around him, drinking from his own long-necked bottle.

"The pride of *Los Mexicanos*." Mr. Cuellar saluted her with his bottle in the air.

The three men with Mr. Cuellar tipped their bright, red plastic cups in the air in salute. Foam spilled over a cup.

Oh, oh. Time to get worried.

"This here girl is gonna whip the asses off all those *gringos*." Mr. Cuellar thumped the air with his cup.

"You show 'em for us," the other men chorused.

Time to get the heck away.

"In two weeks, she's gonna win and show all those fucking *masa* boys who's got what. She's gonna show them that us Chicanos got balls. *¿Qué no, niña?*"

Before Luz could answer, Mrs. Cuellar stepped into the group. "Leave the girl alone."

Too late. Trouble has arrived.

"*¿Qué?* I'm only telling her we want her to win. To show these gringos that us Chicanos can be smart too. Manela, isn't that what you want?"

I'll just take a few steps back and get out of their way. Maybe even disappear.

Mrs. Cuellar positioned her small frame underneath his nose, her body as thin as a flute standing in front of a cello. "Vicente, don't you dare. Luz is going for the women. She's going to prove that we can be leaders as good as any man."

What are they thinking? I'm just one little girl.

Mr. Cuellar commandeered the space around himself, standing taller, puffing out his chest, forcing his wife to step back. "*La Raza.* We have to present a united front. We go as one or we don't make it. Luz is going to win for *La Raza.*" Mr. Cuellar yanked Luz between them, placing his hands on her shoulders.

I'm dead.

Mrs. Cuellar grabbed Luz's hands and tugged the girl forward.

I'm dead for sure.

"Luz is going to win. She has to, but only to prove that Chicanas are just as smart as the men." Mrs. Cuellar's complexion glowed the same warm plum as her lipstick.

Híjo, when they get mad, they turn the same color.

Mr. Cuellar jerked Luz backed closer to him. "Luz has to win to make all *Raza* look good."

I just want to win a spelling contest.

Mrs. Cuellar pulled Luz forward, closer to her. "All you care about is that people believe you men have the biggest balls."

I hope my *abuelita* didn't hear that.

Luz's eyes ping-ponged between the man and the woman. Her head followed the words going over it, her hair swishing back and forth.

Mr. Cuellar pointed a stubbed fingernail at his wife over Luz's right shoulder. "All you're talking is *gringa's* crap. Women's rights are for the whites. My mother was happy taking care of her family. As it should be."

I'm going to get killed in the middle of their fight.

Mrs. Cuellar poked the air over Luz's left shoulder with a red-tipped finger. "*Jodido*, your mother never knew where her husband was at any given moment."

Now they're swearing. My *abuelita* is gonna be angry.

Luz's mother plucked her from between the couple.

Luz's father wrapped his arm around Mr. Cuellar's shoulder and steered him to the grill. "*Compadre*, I need your help with the ribs."

Mrs. Ortíz clutched Mrs. Cuellar's arm and walked away. Both shot scowls at the remaining men. The men raised their hands in defense and backed away.

Luz's mother gripped her arm. "I told you not to cause any trouble."

"But *Mamá*, I was just..."

"Enough. Put your brother to bed. I have to stay in the kitchen."

I wasn't doing anything and I'm the one that gets into trouble. Yeah, being a kid is a whole bunch of fun.

Her mother reached for the sleeping child from the *comadre* who was holding him. Lifting the child's head, she gently lay him on Luz's arm. Luz slipped her other arm close to her mother's body and cradled the child's bottom. Immediately, her mother walked across the yard to rescue someone from Mrs. Cuellar's tirade. Luz carried her brother to the bedroom, soothing him with soft noises. *Qué cariño.*

Luz pulled back the blanket in the crib. One hand under his head and the other under his bottom, she lifted the child over the railing and lay him down in the crib. She tucked the blanket around the child's body, making sure her brother had the pacifier in his mouth. She patted his back until he fell asleep again. There, there, little one, enjoy your dreams while you can. Before the grown-ups start in on you.

Through the window, she watched the people enjoying themselves in her parents' backyard.

Her *Tía* Gloria was biting into a corn-on-the-cob. She wanted Luz to open doors for other Mexican-Americans.

Her *Tío* Ambrose danced a *cumbia*. He wanted her to be safe from a dangerous world.

Her grandmother watched the dancing. She wanted her to get married.

Mrs. Ortíz and Mrs. Cuellar jabbed the chest of a man. They wanted her to be a Chicana feminist revolutionary.

Mr. Cuellar stood next to the grill. He wanted her to change the world for *La Raza*.

Ana danced with both arms wrapped around the neck of Ricardo. Her girlfriends wanted to stay in their world of being smartly one step behind.

Her mother sat with the ladies at the big wooden table. She wanted her to go on to college.

Her father stacked food hot off the grill onto trays. He wanted her to win because it was her obligation and duty as a Chicana.

Luz pressed her hot forehead against the cool window pane. She felt the beat of the music through the window. Loud, rhythmic, vibrant. So many words. Revolution. *La Raza*. Family obligation.

"What you doing here all along, *prima*?"

Luz answered her cousin without looking at her, recognizing the voice. "Putting my brother to bed." *Híjo*, she's lucky. Aura has our grandmother's name and wears a black felt reservation hat just like her.

Aura moved to the other side of the window. "The relatives. Putting on the pressure, *¿qué no?*"

Luz sighed. I want a hat just like that.

"You know they all love you."

"So much love is heavy to carry."

Aura studied her cousin for a few moments then leaned against the wall. "You know I'm the first ever in my family to go to college. So the family expects great things from me."

Luz whipped her head around. "Don't start on me too."

"I wasn't. I was just..."

"I can't tell my elders anything, but you. Forget it."
Luz surprised herself at the anger in her voice, her
hands in fists. "Everybody's telling me what they
want. I would like to do the things they want me to
do. I would like to be a revolutionary. I would like to
win. But..." Luz shook her head. "I don't know if I can.
I don't think I have that kind of courage." She lowered her voice. "I mean I've never gone hungry. My
parents have always given me everything I've wanted." Luz straightened and stretched her hands in
front of her. "I mean, I've never even known a migrant
worker. Who am I to be representing *La Raza*?" There.
I've said it. So shoot me.

Aura looked out the window for a moment, and
almost as if she were speaking to someone outside,
said, "Being *raza* is an attitude."

Luz shook her head as if to disturb the pesky
thoughts. "Then maybe I just have the wrong attitude." Wrong attitude. Wrong color. Wrong
everything.

"Whether you are a winner, light enough, rich
enough, even poor enough, whatever, because you
were born *raza*, the system will never let you forget it.
Every time someone like you or me pushes on this
door that is trying to keep us shut out, it's good."
Aura used her head to indicate everyone at the party.
"But they never got the chance, even though it's the
system that put up the roadblocks."

"You talking about racism?" I know things, too.

"Racism. Genocide. Oppression. Whatever name
you put on it, it's real. It's out there. And that's why it

will be different for you than it will be for the white girls you compete with. No one is going to kill them for trying."

Mrs. Ortíz stuck her head into the room. "Luz, come outside. There is something for you."

Hijo, don't they ever let up?

The three women stepped out into the backyard. Everyone had assembled on the driveway. Mrs. Ortíz steered Luz to the table where the stereo had been turned off. In front of the group, her parents waited for her.

Hijo, I must be in major bad trouble. I always get blamed for everything.

Everyone applauded and cheered, calling out Luz's name over and over. Her father raised his hand for quiet.

"Luz, everyone is very proud of what you've done. We all got together and pitched in to buy you..." her father choked on the words.

Wow! I've never seen my dad like this.

Men and women assembled on the grass shouted words in fun.

"*¡Órale!*" "Hand it to her already."

"*Ya, es tiempo.*"

"Here. This is for you from all of us." Her father handed her a box with a yellow ribbon tied around the middle.

"For me?" Luz put her hands to her face. She looked at the crowd, then back down at the box.

"Open it," was shouted from several in the group. She twisted and yanked the yellow ribbon off the box and ripped the paper off. She lifted the lid and gasped. "*¡Díos mío!* I can't believe my eyes."

"Show us. Show us," came from the group. From the Styrofoam nest, she lifted an electronic dictionary and speller. The instrument fit on her hand. The keyboard filled the bottom space and the wide LED readout tilted up. Her father pointed. "These buttons help you find the word in Spanish, French, or German."

"Only one of those counts," shouted *Tío* Ambrose as he raised his red plastic tumbler and everyone laughed.

Luz grinned. This *familia* is a roller coaster.

Her parents stood on either side of her. Her father squeezed her with his arm around her shoulders; her mother clutched her other arm. "We are all so proud of you."

The clapping and the cheering died off as Mrs. Ortíz and Mrs. Cuellar stepped forward. "We have something for you also."

Hijo. Where can I run?

Luz gingerly set the electronic speller down on the table and then eyed the woman. Mrs. Ortíz shoved a large, rectangular box into her hands.

Her father held the box with both hands as Luz slipped the wide blue ribbon and foot-wide bow from the box. She set the box down on the table and flipped the lid up with one hand. She gasped, as she let the lid fall backwards.

Her parents edged forward. Olga and Ana stretched on tiptoes to get a better view. The cheering audience quieted, holding their breaths, watching.

From the box, Luz lifted an organdy flowered dress with a bright blue sash around the waist. She held it up for everyone to see. Family and friends clapped and hooted and shouted. A bit of green came over Ana's face as she ogled the dress and smacked her lips. Aura gave her a thumbs-up signal. *Abuelita* pushed her wide-brimmed hat to the back of her head, her smile cracking her face into a thousand more wrinkles.

Mrs. Ortíz and Mrs. Cuellar grinned and wrapped their arms around each other's waist. "We never said you couldn't look beautiful while you were changing the world."

Familia. They can make you crazy and they can give you what it takes to get ahead.

Mixing the Ingredients

"*Mamá. Mamá.* Where are you?" Rosaura Ríos sticks her head into the living room. Finding it empty, she moves up the hallway, knocks on the door of her mother's bedroom and opens it. "*Mamá*? I have to talk with you." Empty.

She heads into the kitchen. "There you are."

Her mother is folding clothes at the kitchen table and doesn't look at her.

Rosaura sits at a kitchen chair and shoves a stack of her son's underwear aside. "*Mamá*, Luz said that you told her something bad was going to happen to her if she shows up at the spelling contest." She folds her arms over clothes still warm from the dryer.

Aura pats her grandson's folded pants then places them on the chair to the right with the rest of his clothes.

Rosaura sees the gray and black braid falling down the woman's back, the blue-veined hands, the dark chocolate face, and bites her lip because getting angry with her mother will only make that woman's silence grow. "*Mamá*, I'm sure she just misunderstood you. Didn't she? This is San Antonio, not the wilds."

Her face is as wrinkled as a crumpled paperbag. Aura snaps the baby's crib sheet in the air. "No."

Slender and dark, Rosaura, in her white hospital uniform, grips her hands. "My oldest thinks there's a curse on her, *Mamá*. How could you?"

Without looking at her daughter, Aura asks, "How can you let her go?"

AURA:

Holding their hands, I walked each of my children to school on their first day. Their smiles were as shiny as the new sharp pencils and new blank notebooks they carried in their backpacks.

I stood and watched my daughter walk across the ocean of a yard to the glass doors that were jammed with children pushing their way inside. She was so tiny and looked even smaller as she moved away.

I could not swallow around the hardness blocking my throat. My chest pushed to catch a breath against the sadness pressing down on it. My child. My baby. So very fragile. She was not ready. She will be changed forever in that building. Tears filled my eyes. Oh, my little one. How I wished I could take the blows for you.

At the door you turned around and waved. I waved back, but you were already inside. I stood, watching the door for a very long time.

"*Mamá*, she wants to go. She's thrilled about going. How can you ruin this for her?"

Aura reaches over and yanks a shirt from beneath the elbows of her daughter. Rosaura catches herself from falling forward.

She stares at her mother. "*Mamá*, you do this all the time to me."

"Now this is about you?"

Rosaura searches the room with bright yellow walls, the pot of *frijoles* on the stove scenting the air with spices and childhood memories. The sink and counter are cleaned spotlessly. Her mother's assistance in keeping the house immaculate and functional is immeasurable. She rejects the thought of what her life would be like if she didn't have her mother's support. She knows that she couldn't hold a full-time night job.

"Isn't it?" Rosaura gets up, opens a cabinet and reaches for a glass. She pulls a pitcher of tea from the refrigerator. The children think their grandmother is as central to this family as her mother had always been to her own.

ROSAURA:

I awoke with the taste of a bad dream in my mouth. I scratched my stomach underneath my brother's T-shirt and walked into the kitchen, searching out the starched skirt of my mother's dress to bury my face in.

My nose noticed first. Nothing cooking. The goosebumps on my arms warned me that it was cold in the house. I padded through the doorway to find the living room just as barren. Down the hallway, in front of my parents' bedroom, I listened. Sobs.

The door swung open. My father sat on the edge of the bed, stooped over, one arm with his elbow on his thigh, his head in his hand, the other hand hitting the bed in a slow, piston-like rhythm: up and down, up and down. He never saw me.

All day, with *tíos* and *tías* running in and out of the house, no one saw me. With the phone ringing and people talking, no one heard me. With the day gone and me still in the T-shirt, no one noticed me. With my mouth closed, filled with questions, no one spoke to me.

I watched. I listened. My stomach growled. I crawled back into bed. My mother was gone.

Rosaura asks, "You want some tea?" Her mother shakes her head. "Please, *Mamá* explain." Rosaura sits.

Aura draws back and looks down at her daughter. "Now I have to explain myself for everything."

Aura cocks her head in a pose that reminds Rosaura of a similar look her oldest daughter, Luz, puts on to feign disbelief. Rosaura sighs. "No. Just why did you tell Luz she was in danger?"

"You won't like it." Aura shakes her head, emphasizing the accuracy of her words.

Rosaura slides down in the chair, in a position that earns her daughters a lecture on future slouched spines. "I already don't like it, so what's the difference."

Aura hesitates, then says, "There will be some that will be jealous of her. There will be others that will say things about her. This world," she swings her hand to suggest everyone outside their home, "does not like it when we step out of our place."

AURA:

I was a young woman working a job I did not like, but it kept me home with the children in the day. I cooked *tortillas* at a restaurant until one night the *migra* came and rounded up all those that looked *mexicano*. They would not let me show them my birth certificate. They would not let me call home. They took us to Mexico—all expenses paid, they said.

It had taken me a long time to come home. A long time before I saw my angels again.

Rosaura feels astonished by her mother's attitude. "You saying she shouldn't do this contest because she might get hurt?"

"Will be hurt."

"*Mamá*, in this world, the way it's set up; we have to take risks."

"I know about these risks you talk of."

"Oh, *Mamá*, it's not like when you were young. Some things are easier. We're fighting for more rights."

"So your brain thinks I know nothing of this fight?"

"No." Rosaura hangs tightly onto the table to avoid falling over the cliff of her mother's disdain.

"It is not in the history books that your daughters bring home from school, but it was us," she points to herself, "old Latinas, that picketed the pecan factories and made changes happen." The skirt in her hand suffers an extra hard tug as Aura reminisces. "Your grandfather was a good man and understood. There were others that did not. They walked away from their wives in shame because the women wore pants to stand on the picket lines."

Rosaura stares at the woman whose black, felt reservation hat sits on the back of her head and whose unlit brown *cigarillo* hangs from between pinched lips. The image of the mother she had grown up with. "*Mamá*, you have to be the most outrageous woman I have ever known. I've always been afraid that I couldn't grow up to be the kind of mother you were to us. To be half as strong as you were. You were always there making sure we were treated right."

ROSAURA:
I was in third grade and these boys were picking on me and my girlfriends. Alejandro fought them and he had been taken to the principal. My mother showed up and stood in the front office until, finally, the principal escorted her into his office.

We sat there for three thousand centuries before she left his office. Alejandro was permitted back in school the next day.

Aura puts her hands on her hips. "And what thanks did I get for that?"

Rosaura stares wide-eyed. "I've always appreciated what you did."

"Me and the mothers of your wild girlfriends, we showed up everyday at the big houses on the hill. We cleaned them good, to show those people that we are not dirty." Aura glares from behind lacy underwear.

"We fight, too. We fight to be treated with respect. But that is of no importance for you and your wild girlfriends to think about."

"Of course what you did was important. That's why it's just as important to let Luz go to this competition."

Aura's hand runs down the length of a sleeve slowly. "It is not the same thing. No, it is not. Luz is too young. She is not prepared for what people will say. Do."

Rosaura feels a tenderness grow in her heart towards her mother. "Did many people give you a hard time about the things you wanted?" she asks softly.

Aura lays the blouse on a small pile, then reaches for a towel, snapping it in the air with a loud pop. "Such silly talk. The only time people say things to me is when you left with your wild girlfriends to go to that place." She snatches up the laundry basket and, perching it on one hip, walks to the screen door.

"Ay, *Mamá*, not that again."

Rosaura observes the slight stoop to her mother's shoulder as she walks, yet her head is still held queen high. Her mother pushes the screen door open, steps outside, and disappears to the left. Rosaura can hear her opening the dryer.

Within minutes, her mother is back at the table with another load of dried clothes.

Rosaura speaks quietly into the space her mother has tried to forget. "You've never forgiven me for going against your wishes."

"That's what you say."

"What else am I supposed to think? We've never talked about it. You go stony quiet when I try to bring it up."

Aura shakes her granddaughter's blue blouse and lays it on the ironing board.

"See. You go silent on me. I've never met anyone that can hold a grudge for as long as you can."

ROSAURA:

I filled out the art school applications on Manela's typewriter at her home. I had been accepted at several colleges. With my three girlfriends, I had sneaked away and visited the campuses before Aura had found out.

"You're not going."

"*Mamá*, how can you say this?"

"Easy. See me. You are not going."

I had stomped my feet. "Yes, I am. I've already been accepted."

"And what money are you going to use?"

"I've applied for federal aid and filled out forms for a few student loans."

"I told you not to wear those bell-bottoms in the house."

"I'm talking about my future, my life and you want me to change my clothes."

"You don't see none of those other good Catholic girls wearing those kind of pants. They make you look funny. Fat."

"You don't see their mothers wearing an old Indian hat either."

"Rosaura, no talking like that in this house."

"You don't allow anything in this house. I'm eighteen. I can do what I want."

"Not when you're living in this home of mine."

"That's easy. Consider me gone."

I moved out and rented a place with Manela Cuellar and Marieta Ortiz, my best girlfriends. College had been fun and hard. The male teachers had told me that there was no market for Mexican folk art. I should learn how to paint real art—If I could learn how to paint like a man, that is. The government cut the budget and the money ran out. I was working a full-time job as a waitress when I met my husband.

Aura accuses her daughter, "You have never valued the old ways. You and your wild girlfriends talk about revolution. Talk about changing the world. You forget the importance of tradition. Tradition has its place in a home."

"Not if tradition means letting the man dictate what I can and can't do."

"See, you do not listen. You talk before I am finished and never let me say what I am trying to..."

"I do not. I always hear you out..."

Aura holds the baby diaper half-folded against her chest and stares at her lovely daughter.

Rosaura sits back, smiling. "Oops."

Aura holds back a smile.

Rosaura takes a sip of her tea. "Okay, I'll shut up till you're finished." Aura raises an eyebrow. "I promise." Rosaura crosses her heart. "And hope to die."

AURA:
This one has always been the one that could make me smile.

When she was first born, we weren't sure if she was going to live. Her father had two jobs so it had been left up to me to save the sweet child's life. I went for many days without sleep. There was no doctor that we could go to; only certain doctors would treat *mexicanos*. The *curandera* used all of her knowledge to help my little one stay alive. She was helpful. But still it seemed that God was calling his littlest angel back to him. I vowed that I would never cut her hair if she got well.

Una amiga cleaned the house of a white woman who was a nurse. She risked her job to ask the woman if she could come and see my child. The woman did. She gave medicine, visited often, and Rosaura was able to suck at my breast. This woman, who rarely spoke to her housecleaner, saved my daughter.

"I have nothing to say." Aura clamps her mouth shut.

"See. That's what you always do." Rosaura waves her hands in the air. "First you accuse me of interrupting you; when I try to stop, you back off."

Aura is all innocence. "I do nothing."

"Exactly. You do nothing. You've done nothing with your life. But always, you are trying to stop others from doing something with their lives."

Aura perks up, surprise on her face. "How can you say that? Your brother Alejandro is teaching. He lived here when he went to college. Your sister has a nice job. I watch her children after school."

"*Ay*, a secretary. Where they think it's an accomplishment if she can open the door without hitting her nose." Rosaura shakes her head. "Secretaries are considered lower than shit."

"Everyday she dresses up nice for work and she doesn't have to clean another's toilet. She is a success."

"Right." Rosaura rubs her forehead. "Then there's me."

"Always you put the words in me."

"*Mamá*, when people ask you what I do, what do you tell them?" Rosaura waves her hand in the air.

"That you work hard and are good with your children."

"What about my art?" Rosaura stares, reaching for her mother's understanding.

Aura shrugs. "These people want to know nothing about how you play."

"You don't understand me." Rosaura takes a long drink from her glass, swallowing the hope that her mother will someday understand her desire to create art.

ROSAURA:

I was ten and riding on the back of one of my cousins. The other cousins watched. They started teasing me, making fun of how small I was. Then they told me that the *migra* would come and get my mother again. I got scared, but I wouldn't cry. They kept it up.

I was angry—angry that my happiness was all wrapped up in you and you could be taken from me so easily. I was your angel, you said. But this angel could wake up in the morning to find that her mother had been spirited away to another country.

I did what anger dictated. I leaned forward and bit into the soft flesh of my cousin's shoulder. He yelled and screamed. My cousins tried to pull me off, but I gritted my teeth and became part of his flesh.

You, my father, and his father came running out of the house. The whiny Alfonso had gone running into the house, yelling that I was killing his brother. You pulled me off the boy and held me as my father took *chiles* off the bush near the back door, mashed them between his fingers and rubbed them on my lips.

You held the garden hose over my mouth as I tried to soak out the burn. You asked why I had done it. But I didn't know how to tell you. I needed to be close to you, and you pushed me away. If I wanted to act like a bad girl you had no place on your lap for me.

Aura looks down at her daughter. "Maybe if I knew I would not get blamed for everything that went wrong in your life, it would be easier for me to talk with you. I did the best I could. No one can ask for more." Aura walks to the ironing board, licks her finger and tests the iron.

Rosaura's eyes grow big. "When did I ever ask for more? My brothers were the ones to get anything. Everything was for them. My sister and I lived in hand-me-downs while they sported new shirts and pants all the time."

"They had things to do. All you wanted to do was smear yourself with the paints." Aura spreads a shirt on the ironing board and sprays the sleeve with a bottle of water.

"And that was doing nothing?"

"Tell me how this art helps pay the bills. You are so lucky you have a husband that puts up with you."

"Puts up with me! He's lucky he's got me."

"Always you were the one with the head that could get stuck in a doorway." Aura leans forward. "You have always talked about how bad it was for you, but you never think how it could be for someone else in this family."

AURA:

My husband had taken Alejandro to the bathroom. He couldn't wait until we got home. That one could never wait for anything in his life. You and your sister had your noses pressed against the window, looking at a doll. She was tall, with blue eyes and blond ringlets. You were busy staring at the doll, so you did not notice the paint set above your head. The box sat on its side on a shelf with a picture of all the colors that were inside. Paint brushes, thin ones and thick ones, were lined up in the picture. My fingers itched to feel the brush in my hand, the paint flowing through my fingers.

You and your sister cried. You whimpered all the way home. You had the hiccups bad from sobbing so much. You screamed that I didn't know how bad you wanted that doll.

Rosaura perches on the edge of her chair. "Oh, I guess you're going to tell me that my saint of a sister had it worse than me and I'm the one that always complains."

Aura grins. "You are the one here talking *¿qué no?*"

Rosaura leans forward, shortening the distance between herself and her mother. "*Mamá*, that's not fair. I have tried hard to please you all my life, but nothing I do makes you happy. You've had a complaint about everything I've done. You found something wrong with whatever I did." Rosaura drops back into the chair.

"Is it so bad wanting your daughter to be the best that she can be?" Aura moves the iron down the length of the cloth.

"How about accepting your daughter for who she is?"

ROSAURA:

The Texas sun had melted the sky a pale blue, scorching everything underneath. Pregnant. I felt the heat wave worst. My hair hung to below my waist and my back was wet with sweat. Every time I brushed my hair back, I left it streaked with paint. Finally I tied my hair at my neck, but when I leaned over, my hair fell forward and dipped into the paint. I wanted to cry. Screaming would be better. Instead I reached for the phone.

"Marieta. Get your butt over here right now. I can't fit behind a steering wheel and you're taking me to the beauty shop."

While we were at the beauty shop, a baseball-sized hailstorm hit the city. Marieta took it as an omen from heaven for what was going to happen when I sneaked back into the house.

My children didn't notice. My husband studied me, puzzled, then shook his head and continued eating supper. My mother touched the ends of my hair just below my ears and walked out. She missed supper. We didn't speak to each other for a week.

Aura takes the *cigarillo* out of her mouth. "What about a daughter accepting her mother for who she is? You have not been happy with me for a long time now."

Rosaura stirs uneasily in her chair. "*Mamá*, that's not true. It was you that gave me the courage to go on to college."

"Then I'm sorry about that." She pops the *cigarillo* back into her mouth.

"See, that's what I mean. When it's something you want me to do, everything is fine. But when it's something I want to do, I am wrong."

"No, not wrong. Misplaced maybe."

"Misplaced? How?"

"You are a mother. You have a family to take care of. They are your responsibility. If you wanted to paint and become rich in New York or like that, then you should have kept your knees together." Aura slips the shirt onto a hanger and hooks it on the doorjamb.

"*Mamá*, you just don't understand. All you have ever had in your life is being a mother. It's all you have ever wanted to do. You just don't know what it feels like to have this passion building up inside of you, exploding through your fingers. I have to paint. Sometimes I feel like I'll die if I don't paint." Rosaura holds her hands in front of her, reaching for understanding.

Aura points to herself and shakes her head. "You think this old woman has never had this passion you talk about?"

"*Ay, Mamá*, I know we are your passion. You love us more than life. But this is something different. I know it isn't your fault. In your time, women weren't at liberty to be anything but mothers. Nowadays, things are different. Women can have careers and still be good mothers."

"So you understand why I had no passion in my life." Aura's voice softens.

AURA:

The kitchen was clean. Lunches were set up for the morning rush out the door to school. Laundry was folded and put away. My husband's clothes were pressed and ready for the next morning's job. In their bedrooms, my sons wrestled with their blankets in their sleep. I straightened the blanket on one son, and on the other, I tucked his foot back under the sheet. My daughters were sleeping, hugging stuffed bears tightly in their arms. I removed the flashlight from under the covers where Rosaura had been reading. I smoothed the blankets and stroked the cheek of my littlest rebel.

The doors were locked. The children were asleep. My husband slept soundly. All was quiet in the house. I crept up to the linen closet and reached behind the towels and pulled out a sketch pad. The charcoal were stubs; I was hardly able to hold them in my fingers. I almost had enough saved to buy another box. I sat down and sketched.

Sometimes the neighbor's rooster would let me know that I had been drawing all night.

I hid the sketch pad and the box of charcoal in the linen closet before the family rose. Again I could face the day after letting the passions flow from my fingertips.

Rosaura spreads her hands open. "It's nothing to be ashamed of. Women of your generation had more restrictions put on them than women of today have. Everybody knows that."

"So does this make it easier for you now?"

"No. Not easier."

"Better then."

"Not exactly."

"How come this career is so important if it makes your life even harder?"

"Not harder."

"You blame me for not understanding and you cannot even explain what you do."

"*Mamá*, you're not letting me say what I mean."

Aura sets the iron down, folds her arms and stares at her daughter. "So go ahead and explain. I'm listening."

"Oh, yeah, I can tell you're real receptive to what I have to say."

"I have ears. I'll listen. You want more, prove it to me."

Rosaura sighs. "These days, women want more. They want to prove themselves as good as anyone else. It's the challenge, I guess you could say. To have something to show for themselves at the end of their lives."

"And children are not enough?" Aura looks as if any answer will be the wrong answer.

"No, *Mamá*, children are gifts, on loan to us to take care of for a while. They have their own lives to live and, as their parents, it's our job to raise them to leave us." Rosaura plants both feet on the floor, centering her thinking.

"Then you forget about them?" Aura reaches for a hanger.

"Of course not. Children are worthwhile, but what I'm talking about is something no one else can take credit for except myself. Something of my own. Something like the spelling bee."

"This wasp means the same thing for Luz?"

"Bee, *Mamá*. Spelling bee." Rosaura taps her thighs with her hands. "Yes, it's important. Very important."

"Can you tell how?"

"It will give her a sense of directing her own life." Rosaura holds one hand in the other to add weight to her words.

"She doesn't know which way to go? Tell her to look at the stars."

"*Mamá*, this competition will teach her that she can go for anything she wants. It's not even the winning or losing. It's the showing up that counts."

"I remember saying to you those same words."

"When? I don't remember." Rosaura looks puzzled.

Aura smiles. "I think sometimes you and I have different memories of the same thing."

ROSAURA:

"It's really very simple."

"If it is so simple then why do you have to use so many words?"

"Because you keep interrupting me."

"First you say I don't talk enough, now you say I talk too much. Which one is it?"

"*Mamá*, this boy likes me. He wants to take me to a dance. It's a really important dance. The best dance of the whole year. It's like everyone in the whole school will be there. Anybody who doesn't show up will be an outcast for the rest of the school year." I gulped for air. "Manela and Marieta are going. Even Helen's got a date. And no one is going with their brother. Why do I have go with Alejandro and his date?"

I waited for a response. None came. I stomped my foot. "*Mamá*, why do I have to go with Alejandro?" Still no answer. "*Mamá*, have you been paying attention to me?" I touched her arm.

She looked up from her sewing. "I do not interrupt."

"All right. I can never have anything I want. Everything has to be your way. Cool. I will live with you forever because I'm going to die an old maid. No one will ever want to marry me. Ever." I slammed the door to my bedroom hard. Then I opened the door and slammed it shut again to make my point.

Rosaura chuckles. "Wouldn't surprise me. Sometimes I think I grew up in another house than the one you remember."

AURA:

I was sitting with my sewing when you had come home from school. Alejandro had just told you that you would be going on a double date with him to the school dance.

"It's really very simple."

"If it is so simple then why do you have to use so many words?"

"Because you keep interrupting me."

"First you say I not talk enough, now you say I talk too much. Which is the one it is?"

I watched how you got so excited when you talked. "*Mamá*, this boy likes me." Your eyes were big and the blood rushed in your face. Your skin was darker. "It's a really important dance." I could always tell it was important because you made your forehead all wrinkles when you were really serious. "Anybody who doesn't show up will be an outcast for the rest of the school year." Always many words to say simple things. "And no one is going with their brother." Your whole life was in everything you said. "Why do I have go with Alejandro and his date?"

I didn't say anything. What could I say to make you understand and at the same time not frighten you? You stomped your foot. "*Mamá*, why do I have to go with Alejandro?" Your brother had told me how he heard there might be a fight. *Pachucos* with guns. "*Mamá*, have you been paying attention to me?"

I looked up from my sewing. "I do not interrupt."

"All right. I can never have anything I want. Everything has to be your way." I didn't want you to go, but Alejandro promised to keep you safe. "Cool. I will live with you forever because I'm going to die an old maid." How could I let you go into the world and keep you safe, too? "No one will ever want to marry me. Ever."

You slammed the door twice; my sewing fell from my lap. You didn't talk to me the rest of the time before the dance. The night of the dance I sat in the dark, listening to the radio, drawing how beautiful you looked. When I heard the car, I checked in the window and saw how that good boy, Isidro, walked you to the door. I hurried to bed.

Rosaura sits in silence, watching her mother iron. "I was little and sitting in this kitchen, watching you just like you are now. I remember telling you that I would die if anything happened to you."

"Like I died when you were in college and I never knew how you were or where you were?"

"*Ay*, we're back to that again." Rosaura pops out of her chair, stomps to the kitchen sink, rinses her glass and drops it in the dish rack. "*Mamá*, don't be telling Luz any more of your stories."

Aura slows the stroke of the iron.

"She's young. She believes everything you say and you frightened her. She doesn't need it."

Aura stares at the wall ahead of her.

Rosaura glances at her mother's back. "She's having a tough time with this competition. The things that are important to us are not the same things that are important to you."

ROSAURA:

I was eight and there was this big, brown dog with big fangs that I had to pass every day on the way to school.

I ate my breakfast slow, searched for the right books to pack, and was the last to leave in the mornings. You scolded me every day for a week. Then on Monday morning, you told my brothers and sister to go on ahead of me. I thought you were going to beat me. They did, too. My brothers teased me. I wanted to cry.

Instead, you took me by the hand and led me into the living room. You sat on your padded rocking chair and told me to get on your lap. You wrapped your arms around me and rocked me for a very long time. Very softly, you were humming a tune. I could hardly hear it. After the ball in my stomach unraveled, I asked you to tell me what you were humming. You said you would tell me only if I told you what was the thing that was making it hard for me to get to school in the morning.

I went silent. You kept humming that tune and holding me tight. Soon I was sobbing, telling you about the big, brown dog with the huge teeth. You kept holding me tight.

You walked me to school that day and let me hide behind your skirts when we passed the house with the dog. You whispered in my ear when you left me off at the front of the school that you had been afraid of the dog, too.

After that, each morning my brothers walked me by the house with the dog. Several days later, I thought it was curious when I saw you leaving that house. You pretended that you had been standing on the sidewalk, waiting for us. You smiled and walked with us the rest of the way home. Then the dog disappeared. I never knew why.

Aura turns slowly and glares at her daughter. "Wanting the children to be safe is not important to you?"

Rosaura shifts uncomfortably under the weight of her mother's gaze. "If you can tell me how to make it one hundred percent safe for Luz in the world we live in today, I'll do it."

"Don't let her go."

Rosaura grips the table. "For her to be safe and at the same time, be able to reach for whatever star she wants."

Aura studies her daughter. "You have no fear for her? Of those who will do anything to keep her in her place?"

"I worry about her all the time."

Aura cocks her head.

Rosaura explains, "Fear is what they are counting on to keep us down."

"Who is they?"

"Society. The power structure. Economics."

"You will let your daughter be among these theys if they are the ones wanting to hurt her?"

"It's where the action is. It's where she has to succeed to get anywhere. You see *Mamá*, I trust Luz to be smart enough to know what's real and what's not. That's why I've talked to her so much about oppression and all the 'ism's. If she can't make it through this one thing, I haven't done a good enough job. Hopefully, I've taught her to be strong in herself so she can do what she wants to do."

"And you going to college..."

"Was because you raised me strong. You raised me to believe in myself. You taught me I was lovable and that's what gave me the strength to believe in myself."

"Even if it breaks the heart of your mother."

"Oh, heck, we're right back to where we started. Facing white people was easier than living with the guilt trips you put on me."

Aura lets her shoulders drop then unplugs the iron. She walks out of the room pulling her black felt reservation hat down over her eyes.

"*Mamá*, I'm sorry. I didn't mean it quite that way." Rosaura speaks to an empty doorway.

"*Mamá*," Rosaura says, looking down the hallway, watching her mother enter the bedroom.

AURA:

I shake my head in sadness. Maybe someday my daughter will come around and see that what I have to say has some value. Maybe someday she'll realize that what I care most about is the way she lives her life, and the way I live mine. I just do what I have to do.

ROSAURA:

I shake my head in sadness. Maybe someday my mother will come around and see that what I have to say has some value. Maybe some day she'll realize that what I care most about is the way she lived her life, and the way I am living mine. I just do what I have to do.

Kneading Attitude

Rosaura was in her first show at the Sol del Mar Art Gallery.

Weeks before, Marieta had approached the director who had conceived the show spotlighting new artists in the San Antonio area, "Treasure Hunt: Discovering the City's Hidden Talent." She had shown Mr. Richardson Rosaura's slides. She had talked and talked, not waiting for a pause, not letting him say "no," only stopping when he laughed. She had stared, her eyes hardening to small black coals. He said he'd allowed the panel of jurors to consider the slides and, after he did, the panel accepted them. After Marieta notified the press of the gallery's choices and the announcements had been sent, the opening arrived on a typically hot Texas day.

Mr. Richardson trailed after Marieta into the hallway and touched her shoulder. His light brown hair was streaked blonde after his vacation at his wife's summer home in Aspen. He was taller than Marieta, his body sculpted from daily workouts at the Gold's Gym. Usually dressed in a sports coat and open collar shirt, today he wore a dark power suit for the gallery's opening.

Marieta had overheard Mr. Richardson tell a co-worker that he liked what he saw in her, a small frame decorated in dark brown skin. Her hair moved with just a touch of bounce, the same bounce, he had chuckled, that matched the movement under her skirt as she walked away. Mr. Richardson and the co-worker had laughed together.

Now, Mr. Richardson stepped near and ran his knuckles along her hair, his fingers skimming her cheek as she pulled away. "Tell me. Do Rosaura's eyes blaze as full of passion and fire as yours?"

Marieta sighed. Another *gringo* pigeonholing her into their stereotype of hot Latinas. She walked down the hall, the pressure of his gaze like hot breath on her skin. She would be damned if she was going to let his behavior stop her from being proud of her body.

She reached for the phone at her desk while checking down the hall. Mr. Richardson waved his fingers and gave her a chop-licking smile. She wrapped her fingers around the receiver, leaving the middle finger straight up for him to see, and dialed the phone. He chuckled as he slipped back into his office.

Three hours later, Marieta stood in the gallery. The two fans that hung from the high ceiling rotated slowly to give the illusion of Southern antiquity when air-conditioning took care of temperature and humidity. The lighting was soft and recessed, except for the strip lighting focused on the individual paintings. As footsteps clicked across polished, hardwood floors, the gallery achieved a cathedral-like quality. A variety of paintings lined the walls on either side of the room. Rising from the middle of the room toward the back, facing the entrance, was a panel almost ceiling-high. Rosaura's paintings were on the backside of this panel.

Marieta walked along the wall, stopping once or twice. She felt the swirls and the strokes as if she had done them herself. She would hold her hand close to each canvas and believe she could feel what the artist had felt: the tension, the passion, the joy of each stroke, of each color, colors swimming in union. Take one color, then another, spread the paint one way, then another, think about the overlay of texture, the contrast of color and slowly, with patience, the illusion emerges. The artist's vision.

Several years back, she had asked Rosaura for painting lessons for her birthday. She had cried. She had quit after five classes. Marieta appreciated the labor it took to create good art, but now she worked at displaying other people's art, always aching to paint one of her own pieces. But always there was a moment before each show in which she allowed herself to dream, her and the artwork alone.

Rosaura stepped into the gallery. "I still find it so hard to believe that my work is hanging in a gallery."

Marieta dragged her consciousness back to reality. "And no one else better deserves it than you." She smiled.

Rosaura tugged at her suit. "Do I look all right?"

Marieta skimmed over her best friend, the envy of most with her warm, molasses-brown skin, brown-gold eyes, and blue-black, thick, short hair. Marieta gritted her teeth every time she remembered that Rosaura's hair had been waist length. The dumbest thing Rosaura had ever done as far as she was concerned. "*Chula*, you're perfect. *Órale*, the tea will be in the courtyard, but first let's see how your art looks."

Marieta took Rosaura's arm in hers. They'd been best friends since grade school, through their first bleeding, their high school softball championship game, their late night huddles, their receiving THE first kiss. Marieta Ortíz has always been una amiga to hang low and dirty through the fun times and the clinches. Rosaura had learned how to fistfight because Marieta never backed off from an argument. In the classroom, the teachers had situated them as far apart as possible.

The gallery filled with couples, women dressed in suits nipped and tucked in high fashion. The most daring wore a pale yellow suit; the rest wore a smear of vanilla. Rosaura tugged at her red blazer. In a light rose suit, Marieta jerked Rosaura's hand away and shook her head. The two women were like rain forest flowers floating across a sea of milk.

Five women stood in a semicircle in front of Rosaura's work. Marieta pitched forward to be heard above the conversations around them. "Ladies, I'd like to introduce you to Rosaura Ríos. This is her work." Marieta made a sweeping gesture towards the painting on the wall. "One day you can say you saw her here first." Marieta smiled.

Rosaura nodded at the five women. "I'm so happy to be here. This is a beautiful gallery."

The blonde woman with the Galveston-tan next to Rosaura extended a hand. Rosaura felt relief from the warm response on the woman's face as she shook her hand.

Rosaura stepped forward to allow a couple to walk by, then turned to the woman on her left as Suzan Richardson asked, "How many years have you been painting, dear?"

Marieta knew Mrs. Richardson's silver-colored suit was new for this opening; she had never seen that woman in the same outfit twice. Marieta wished she owned Richardson's closet.

"All my life, I guess. With children, it's a little harder to get the time, but I'm sure y'all understand that." Rosaura smiled.

There was a twitter of laughter from the women. Mrs. Richardson said, "I just have the Mexican girl take the children out."

Two of the women nodded to each other, wide-brimmed hats touching, then leaned forward to hear above the din of the group next to them.

"Rosaura Ríos?" Glancing at the name on the painting then at the woman, the minister's wife, Mrs. Thatcher asked, "Didn't your daughter win the spelling bee last week?"

A group of women maneuvered between them to view the picture. So only Mrs. Whitting heard Mrs. Thatcher say, "She'll be representing the South San District in a week or so, won't she?"

Rosaura beamed. "Yes. I'm so proud of her."

Mrs. Thatcher glanced over at a woman standing at another painting. "Excuse me. I have to go speak with Mrs. Williams. She's the principal's wife and is expecting a report from me." She trotted off, cutting through clusters of people, dropping smiles on them like coins in a collection basket.

Marieta turned her attention to the rest of the women. "Appears the whole family is in the spotlight this week."

Harriet Whitting studied the oil painting of a Latino Christmas event. Three young women sat at a kitchen table, spreading *masa* on corn husks to make tamales, and two older women stood at the stove, stirring a huge metal pot. To Rosaura she said, with a nod to her companions, "Your basic palette is extremely brash. Have you ever experienced the subtle pastels of Monet?" A burst of laughter erupted from the other side of the room.

Rosaura's smile faded.

Marieta grabbed Rosaura's hand and held it tightly.

The other women grouped tighter as three others joined them and angled forward to inspect the painting.

Mrs. Whitting nodded as, with one finger tapping her chin, she studied the piece. "Folk art with a lack of subtlety of value change. Characteristic of art from our neighbors south of the border. When did your family immigrate to America?"

"We have to move on. I have other people that want to meet Rosaura." Marieta tugged at Rosaura, who was already engaged in a staring battle with Mrs. Whitting.

"My family became Americans when Texas was annexed just after my great-great-grandmother's birthday. We had already been living on this land for several decades before the white people, your people, stole this country from us."

The woman with the wide-brimmed hat glanced at her neighbor. They touched brims again and rolled their eyes. The new arrival to the group sensed the tension and moved on, calling out to a friend.

Rosaura said, "I'm fifth-generation American. What generation are you?"

Mrs. Whitting put her gloved hand to her breast. "I was merely trying to make conversation. I didn't realize you would be so sensitive."

Rosaura turned to leave with Marieta when the woman who had shaken her hand said, "Your art is masterful. Alive. Pulsing with energy. If this gallery was smart they'd keep you in their stable of artists. I'm eager to see more of your work exhibited throughout the city." The woman slipped her a business card. "Call me. I can make that happen."

Rosaura bowed her head quickly at the woman, then let Marieta lead her to the courtyard.

Outside, the Texas sun did its best against a cloth of blue sky to sizzle everything underneath. From above, high windows and iron filigree balconies with flowering vines climbing up the walls, looked down on the courtyard. A splashing fountain, adorned in blue and white tiles, squatted in the middle of the courtyard; water drops played their song softly. A faint rainbow arched across the top of the fountain.

Standing in the courtyard, with paper-thin slices of cheese on wafers that crumbled when bitten, the women sipped from blue-flowered china cups. Caterers rushed back and forth, filling platters and silver urns. Waiters roamed, on the lookout for empty cups or plates to fill with bite-sized delectables. People mingled, snaking from one group to another. Conversations were soft-toned in one group, boisterous in another. Plastic smiles nodded to boring conversationalists, while artists networked. With one arm behind her back, Rosaura shook her jacket to let some air cool her sweaty back. But in spite of the heat, all the other women appeared non-plussed.

Rosaura whispered to Marieta, "These ladies don't sweat?"

Marieta handed Rosaura a glass of wine. "They don't sweat, *Chula*. They perspire." Marieta exaggerated the word. "But I've seen them with armpits as dark as you and me."

Rosaura turned away to keep from barking out a laugh and bumped into Mrs. Mendoza. "Elena, thank God. I was feeling like the only one here."

Helen Mendoza stiffened at her remark. "Helen," she corrected. "Of course, you would as the token artist here." Her smile was as soft as those carved on the marble statues around them. "But I wouldn't despair. Everyone understands." She gave a nod of recognition to Marieta.

Marieta noticed that Helen needed to get her behind to a beauty shop soon, as her brown roots were showing against her lightened hair. Helen's suit of bleached white with a white, pleated handkerchief coming from her breast pocket screamed respectability all the way down to her white high heels. She held her five-feet-four-inches so straight and stiff, Marieta thought the girl looked constipated or as if she had something really stiff up her derrière. Marieta grinned at Helen.

"Let's all sit at the same table. Keep us homegirls together. For protection," suggested Rosaura.

Marieta added, "For whose protection? Theirs or ours?" Rosaura and Marieta slapped palms in midair.

Helen stepped back, head low, scanning the immediate area, surveying whether any of the ladies standing close by had heard the reference to homegirls. "I'm needed at the Board of Directors table. Excuse me." She slipped by them in a rush.

Rosaura stared after her. "Did I say something wrong?"

Marieta put her hand on her friend's shoulder. "You know Elena. Oh, excuse me, Helen. She's got a hair up her ass about being so light-skinned."

"She's still on that kick about being a descendant from Spaniards?"

"As we speak, she's having her family crest bronzed on some shield she's found."

"*Hijo*. I'm going to ask my Justina if Sally Jane is the same way."

"Helen's daughter? I doubt it. She has more important things to worry about."

Marieta and Rosaura butted shoulders and said together, "Boys, boys, and more boys."

They were laughing so hard that a couple of ladies, deep in conversation with Helen, squinted over their shoulders to examine the situation. Helen never looked around.

A hand seized Rosaura's shoulder. "Oh, so here she is." Mr. Richardson took Rosaura's hand in his and patted it with the other. He looked at Marieta and said, "The same eyes as yours." He winked. "I approve wholeheartedly." He took her hand and looped it through his arm. "Let me escort you up front. All the artists are gathering for the introductions."

As he led her away, Rosaura shot a quick glance at her homegirl.

Marieta shooed her on with a hand. "Go on. I have work to do. I'll meet you later."

The afternoon was climbing to a comfortable, Texas ninety-two degrees. After the introductions, the polite clapping from the ladies present, and a loud "órale" from Marieta when Rosaura was awarded the $150 Panel Award, the photographers took over. The snapping and flashing went on for over an hour as patrons skillfully contrived to have their pictures taken with their protégés. People oohed and ahhed as each group took their turn in front of the photographers. Everybody rushed to congratulate the artist who had been awarded the "Best of the Show," wanting to be the first to make an impression.

After Rosaura had her picture taken with her award, she joined Marieta on the sidelines, sitting on a wrought-iron bench.

Mr. Richardson rushed over, took one in each hand and drew them into the fawning crowd. He wrapped an arm around each of their waists and told the photographer to snap him with the dark-horse entry. The two friends smiled their with-white-people-polite smiles as bulbs flashed, until Mrs. Suzan Richardson crooked her finger and Mr. Richardson quickly padded over to her.

As the guests were edging their way out on route to other important social gatherings, Marieta guided her friend through the crowd en route to the ladies room. Dozens of limp kisses floated on the air as patrons signaled good-bye to each other.

Inside the bathroom after checking all the stalls, they burst out laughing. Rosaura held her side. "I'm going to have black and blue marks from where he was pinching me."

"Me, too. How do I explain them to my husband?"

Rosaura grinned. "Don't."

They were still laughing as Rosaura entered a stall. Marieta pulled out her make-up bag.

After they had both dabbed their noses, freshened their lips, and recombed their hair, Marieta grabbed Rosaura by the arms. "*Andale*, let's see your pieces before you leave. I want you to get that this is really for real." She dragged her best friend back into the empty gallery.

The two girlfriends stood with their arms entwined before the prize-winning painting. Marieta squeezed Rosaura's hand and pronounced in an official tone, "The quality of the brush-strokes, the contrast of scale, and the daring choice of color lends to a typical scene of home life in the barrio, a pulsating and other-world regal ambience not often displayed in such an excellent format."

Rosaura looked at her.

"Spiel, girlfriend. What I tell the patrons."

"Oh."

"But between you and me, this stuff is good."

Rosaura smiled. "Stuff, huh?"

"Some hot shit stuff, girlfriend."

From behind them came the words, "My sentiment exactly, but not necessarily the words I would write in the brochure."

The Galveston-tanned woman, who had shaken hands with Rosaura earlier, approached them. "I didn't introduce myself. I'm Mrs. Phyllis Crenshaw." She shook hands with both women. "I like your work. I'm with the Bankman Gallery on San Pedro." Blue-eyed and tall, her blonde hair was cut to soften the angles of her face. Her wide smile brought life into her eyes.

Marieta and Rosaura gripped hands and smiled. Mrs. Crenshaw owned the biggest art gallery in San Antonio.

"I don't want to leave today without confirming a time when you can stop by to see me. I'd like to look over your portfolio." She stopped and Marieta took a breath to squeeze out the shock.

"I'd like to discuss the possibility of continued representation at my gallery."

When Marieta looked at her silent girlfriend, she nudged Rosaura into taking a breath. When Rosaura didn't say anything, Marieta jumped in. "Would you like to go to my desk so we can schedule an appointment? Rosaura's schedule is very busy." As Marieta stepped around the panel, towing a speechless friend by the arm, Mrs. Crenshaw said, "Not necessary. I have my book here. Just tell me if ten Thursday morning would be convenient for you, and I'll write it in."

Before either woman could speak they were surrounded by Mrs. Emily Thatcher, Mrs. Suzan Richardson, and Mrs. Harriet Whitting. Marieta hid her chuckle as she considered the three women—the lion who had wanted courage, the tin man who had wanted a heart, and the straw man who had wanted a brain.

Mrs. Whitting with her hay-colored hair led the group. "Marieta."

Marieta faced the women. "Harriet," she dragged the name out and bowed her head slightly. First-name basis worked both ways, she thought.

Mrs. Whitting smiled as if it had been painted on. Her pale yellow suit hung loosely over her stooped shoulders. "We're very upset."

Mrs. Richardson, her silver hair lacquered into a shiny helmet, swung her clutch bag up and down like an ax. "We just heard something that you may be unaware of."

Marieta looked from woman to woman in confusion.

Mrs. Thatcher licked her lips and nodded in agreement. "We just spoke to the principal's wife," she said.

"I knew there was a reason why your name sounded so familiar to me," said Mrs. Whitting.

"Someone reported her daughter." Mrs. Richardson pointed with her bag at Rosaura. "They say she stole the list of words used at the contest."

Marieta stared at the women, in awe of their blustery self-importance.

Mrs. Whitting puffed up like a broom in a windstorm as Rosaura stepped before her, controlled and aglow. "Why are you making accusations you can't prove?"

The only time Marieta had ever seen her girlfriend this angry was when the both of them had whipped Dolores Fuentes and two of her girlfriends after Dolores accused Rosaura of stealing her boyfriend. Marieta feared that these three uptight ladies didn't stand a tornado's chance in Kansas.

Mrs. Thatcher eased herself behind the two other women. Mrs. Richardson moved beside Mrs. Whitting as she maintained, "Accusations based on facts. Someone came forward with the truth."

Mrs. Whitting pushed her words on Rosaura. "One of your own."

Marieta moved quickly alongside her girlfriend. "One of our what? Human beings? Women? Exactly what is one of our own?"

Mrs. Thatcher pawed the air. "Ladies, this can be resolved in a civilized way."

Mrs. Richardson said, "Don't expect to keep your Panel Award."

Mrs. Crenshaw stepped in front of the two girl-friends. "Excuse me. What does this have to do with her artwork?"

Mrs. Richardson softened her approach in the face of one of her husband's competitors. "We suspect foul play."

"Her daughter is a thief," Mrs. Whitting stated. "How do we know if she didn't do something with this one?" She shot a finger in Marieta's direction. "Maybe they got together and fixed the awards some-how."

Mrs. Crenshaw felt the forward momentum of the two women behind her and blocked their progress. "Suzan, these are severe accusations your friend is making. I would think twice before presuming that your husband's position would absolve you from the consequences of preposterous allegations." She took Suzan Richardson's arm in hers, pulled her away from Mrs. Whitting. As she led her out of the gallery, she said, "Why, I would dread to think of the complaints that could come from such false accusations." She smiled over Mrs. Richardson's shoulder and said to Marieta, "I'll meet you in your office in a few minutes to firm up the time," then continued out of the gallery.

Mrs. Whitting stalked after them, but stopped at the door and looked back over her shoulder. "Don't think you're going to get away with humiliating my daughter."

Helen Mendoza tiptoed around the exiting Mrs. Crenshaw and Mrs. Richardson. "Ladies, is there any trouble?" She took in Marieta and Rosaura, ready to pounce, and encircled Mrs. Whitting with an arm. "Please come with me. Let me get you something to drink."

Mrs. Whitting allowed herself to be ushered out. Mrs. Thatcher looked back, raised her purse, opened her mouth, then changed her mind. She said, "God will light the just path." Then she marched out.

At the door, Helen backed up and blazed a look of disgust at the two women. "You two just couldn't behave yourselves. Some of us have a future to think about for ourselves and for our children." She paraded out.

Marieta grimaced, thinking that her old girlfriend was holding her head at a painful right angle to her heart.

As the women disappeared behind the closing door, Rosaura gripped her friend's hands. "Luz would never cheat. Who could be saying that she did?"

Marieta knew her girlfriend was too angry to cry. That would come later. "Ease up, girlfriend. You know these women will say anything to keep us from moving on."

Rosaura faced Marieta with hope in her eyes. "You think that's it?"

"Of course. Anyone who knows Luz knows that she wouldn't cheat. We'll straighten all this out. For now, we have to meet Mrs. Crenshaw in my office."

"*Ay, Chula*, I can't."

"Why not?" asked Marieta.

"I have to go find Luz. I'm sure she'll be upset."

"But what about your art? What about Mrs. Crenshaw's offer?"

"It'll just have to wait. My child comes first."

"Feeling scared about making it?"

Rosaura stopped on her way to the door and turned around. "What're you getting at?"

"You have a chance of a lifetime and you're letting it go by."

"My child's in trouble. I'm a mother first and..."

"No. You're a woman first. An artist second and then a mother."

Rosaura shook her head and opened her mouth to speak, but Marieta continued, "Your mother is at home when the kids arrive after school, *¿que no?*"

Rosaura nodded.

"Your husband arrives home from work in another hour, *¿que no?*"

Rosaura kept her head stiff.

"Are you trying to tell me that you're the only parent that can care for the children?"

Rosaura didn't nod, the stiffness spilled from the seams. "It's not that. It's..."

"It's *caca*. You're getting a big break and you're running. You're using your kids as an excuse to keep from going out into the real world and being visible. They're hard on us. Harder than what's called for. You're afraid of being visible because that makes you a target."

"*Mira*, you don't understand..."

"No, it's you that doesn't understand." Marieta lowered her voice as she stepped in front of Rosaura's painting. "You have a talent, a gift from God, and you're just letting it slip away. Don't you see?"

"I have my kids and they're my responsibility, too."

Marieta shook her head. "And your kids are well-taken care of and know in their heart, without a doubt, that their mother is there for them whenever they need her. Who is there for you? Who is there for your art?"

Rosaura sighed. "It's not important..."

"Listen, mujer. I saw you drawing on the back of used pieces of notebook paper when we were kids. I watched the art teacher in high school shine on you. I took your slides and fought for the jurors to look at them."

"You know I appreciate what you did for me."

"No you don't. Not if you walk out and don't talk with Mrs. Crenshaw." Marieta walked away.

Rosaura looked from her painting to the door.

"Rosaura."

The changed tone of Marieta's voice caught Rosaura's attention.

"I've never told you. I've never told no one." Marieta paused as she stopped at the door and looked back into the gallery. "I've always envied you. I would give anything if I could paint like you do."

"But you're the one that quit the lessons. I told you that you were improving."

"Improving to what? First-grade refrigerator drawings." Marieta shook her head. "No. I want to paint like you. I want to be able to put my soul out on the canvas like you can. Like no one else can do it quite like you. You tell a story about our lives. You give people a glimpse of what and who we really are—not the stereotypes, but us as real people." She wet her lips. "You have a gift. You owe it to yourself to run with it. You deserve the praise and the glory. You deserve it all." Marieta sighed. "And I'd like to kill you because you're so good and I'm so jealous."

Rosaura stared at her girlfriend. "I didn't know. You never said..."

"What? Rosaura, I hate you because you can do something I love better than me?"

"No, but..."

"I'm not important right now. You are." Marieta pointed down the hallway. "You have to meet with Mrs. Crenshaw. It'll only take a few minutes. You owe it to yourself, to your artwork. And if you want to get on a soapbox, you owe it to all the other Chicana artists to be the best you can be."

"*Híjo.*" Rosaura whispered at the serious expression on her best friend's face. "I didn't know it meant so much to you."

Marieta crossed her arms and tapped one foot. Dropping her head and with eyes rolled up, she stared at Rosaura. "It means so much to me that if you don't go in there and make that appointment, you can forget me in your life."

Rosaura's mouth fell open slowly. "You mean..." She shook her head. "You're not serious..." She pointed at her friend. "You wouldn't really..." She looked away and squared her shoulders. "I might as well go." Rosaura turned away.

"I mean it, girlfriend." Marieta spoke in a low, hard voice. "If you walk away from this opportunity, you can kiss our friendship good-bye."

Rosaura stopped at the door. "I know you're thinking of what's good for me. I know you don't mean it." Memorable escapades littered across her mind as one episode after another reminded her of what they had gone through together.

"Know how much I mean this. If you walk out, you'll never see me again."

Rosaura frowned. "*¿Por qué?* Just because of this?" She waved a hand at the gallery.

Marieta explained, "This is where you have been heading all your life. Your artwork needs to be out in the world. I truly believe this. You have a gift. You throw away this gift, you throw away our friendship."

"What does one have to do with another?"

Marieta swung her hands in front of her. "I don't know. I do know that you have been waiting for this opportunity all your life. There is no way you're going to walk away from this just because you're scared."

Rosaura threw her spine straight, her hands on her hips. "You saying I'm scared?"

"Damn straight." Marieta's chin rose perpendicular to the floor.

Rosaura waved a fist in the air. "I ain't afraid of nothing."

Marieta's chin rose higher. "Prove it."

"I don't have to prove anything to you." Rosaura pressed forward.

"Prove it to yourself." Marieta crowded her.

Rosaura thumped her chest. "I know what I know."

"You've never known anything."

"I was always smarter than you in school." Rosaura sliced the air with her finger.

"No, you weren't."

"Yes, I was."

"No, you weren't."

"Yes, I was."

"No, you weren't."

They looked at each other and burst out laughing. They leaned on each other as they slipped from laughing to giggles back to laughing heartily.

Taking short breaths of air, Rosaura asked, "You're not serious?"

Marieta nodded, attempting to control her giggles.

Rosaura gasped for air then asked, "Why?"

"Because I love you." Marieta straightened and gazed at her friend.

Rosaura explored her friend's brown eyes. "Well, what you going to do?"

Rosaura grinned. "You know, Helen would absolutely shit a brick if she saw me making it."

Marieta laughed. "You know it, girlfriend." They slapped palms in mid-air.

Rosaura turned serious. "*Chula*, are you going to get into trouble here because of me?"

Marieta laughed, put her left hand on her hip, and pointed with one finger downward. "And since when have I needed you to get into trouble? Girlfriend, no one is going to dis one of my own and get away with it."

Rosaura couldn't keep from smiling. "Where did you pick up that word? Dis?"

"The kids were using it in the backyard the other day." Marieta headed for the door of her office.

Rosaura grabbed her by the elbow. "Do you even know what it means?"

Marieta shook her head. "But don't it sound good?"

"Bad."

Marieta looked puzzled. "Why is it bad?"

"No. The kids nowadays call anything good, bad."

"Good. I'll remind you of that when we read what the critics have to say about your art."

Harriet vs. Lyna Lou

"Tell her it's the end of the world."

The maid carried the portable phone to the study. "Mrs. Whitting, someone on the phone for you," said Anita. "He says to tell you it's the end of the world."

The woman at the polished King Louis desk looked up and smiled. She took the phone and spoke to the maid, "Please, dust those bookshelves. I've been sneezing all morning." Then into the phone, she said, "Brody! Where are you? How are you? Are you all right?"

"Whoa. Give a man a chance to say something. I'm fine, I'm fine. I'm still in Houston, working at the community center."

"Oh, Brody you still haven't outgrown that adolescent urge to save the world?" Mrs. Whitting watched the girl do her job. Anita's dark face resembled the gaunt and oval-eyed expression of the wooden carvings from Africa on the shelf next to her.

"Well, someone has to do it."

"But why you? Why for so long? You know you had your pick of New York law firms when you graduated. It would have broken our father's heart if he had been alive to see you walk away from all those offers." Mrs. Whitting stepped up to the bookcase and ran a finger over a dusted shelf.

Anita kept her back to the lady.

"If our father had bothered staying around long enough. But I'm making my *mamá* proud. She was here the other week. Asked about you."

Mrs. Whitting lowered her voice and walked into the foyer. "You didn't tell her where she could find me, did you?"

"I gave you my word. Or does living with all those rich folks make you distrust your kinfolk?"

"Oh, Brody. Why do you speak in that manner?" Her voice raised like a young girl talking to her beau.

"When in Rome, y'know. How are the kids? How're Debbie and Kathy? Beautiful, like their mother?"

"Oh, they're doing fine. Kathy's riding now, did I tell you?" Mrs. Whitting paused at the door of the living room. She scanned the room and was unsatisfied. She walked back to her study.

"What? No glorious comments on the ravishing Debbie?"

"We have a bit of a problem." She crooked her finger at Anita. The maid followed her.

"What? Is she ill? Has she been hurt?"

"In a manner of speaking. Remember, I told you she was competing to represent the South San district at the city-wide spelling bee?"

"Yeah, but I don't see what's the big deal about a spelling bee."

Mrs. Whitting covered the phone. "Anita, make sure those trays are within reach but not too close to the edge. I wouldn't want them to be knocked over. I already explained that to you once." To her brother she said, "It was to her. She lost."

"Hey, that's tough. But it's life. She'll bounce back."

"Brody, she lost to a Mexican girl." Mrs. Whitting looked at her girl. Anita pointed to an almost empty bottle in the liquor cabinet and Mrs. Whitting nodded. "Some girl named Luz Ríos. Such funny names."

"Sis, hate to break it to you, but Chicanos got brains too."

"Have, and don't be condescending."

Anita held the bottle up.

"Who's being rude? I'm stating a fact."

Mrs. Whitting mouthed, "Get a new one," and into the phone she said, "For your information, we've just found out that THAT Mexican girl stole the words used at the competition. I haven't told Debbie yet, but there's a good chance she may still be able to go to Austin."

"The list of words? How could she steal 'em?"

"We both know that they're crafty enough to do anything."

Anita kept her spine straight, her head high and her hands close to her side as she walked to the pantry.

"Oh, yeah, we know because we grew up in the same neighborhood as they did. In fact, when mom was ill, it was Mrs. Torres that kept us out of the clutches of the social workers. But I could be wrong."

"Don't you get high and mighty with me. I'm still your big sister."

"Only by three minutes."

"Three minutes is all it takes."

"Lyna Lou, seriously..."

"Brody, I've told you to call me Harriet."

"Just because you married that rich doctor and changed your name don't make you any less my sister, Lyna Lou Gallagher."

"It's Harriet Whitting."

"So what is the school going to do about the competition?"

"The school board is having a special meeting at South San High School to give Debbie the official okay to represent them at the city-wide competition. Isn't that exciting?"

"What's going to happen to that other girl?"

"How should I know? For that matter, why should I care? She probably stole the words because she's used to having everything handed to her."

"Handed to her?"

"You know. Affirmative action. These minorities are getting lazier by the minute because they know that by crying discrimination, they get everything served up to them on a silver platter."

Anita held up the new bottle and Mrs. Whitting nodded.

Brody said, "Because good respectable people work hard to get their rewards. Only the stupid or weak take handouts."

"Now you're sounding like daddy."

"I know."

"You don't believe it?"

"Lyna Lou, everyday here I see good people suffering…"

"And complaining to you, instead of getting out there and finding a job. If they had any gumption, they would be able to find work."

Mrs. Whitting pointed to a stain on the carpet. Anita stepped to the closet under the stairway and snatched up a Dust Buster to attack the unforgiven spot.

"That's right," said Brody. "I'm talking to the person that worked everyday after school and on weekends."

Mrs. Whitting stepped out of earshot of the maid. "You know that all our classmates never let me forget that I only had two dresses to wear. That sometimes you had to go to school barefoot. You had more fights because you wouldn't let anyone laugh at us. You mean to say, you've forgotten all that?"

"Not so much forgotten, but forgiven. It just isn't so important anymore. I work with people that have even less than we did."

"Oh, the poor minorities." Mrs. Whitting slipped past Anita as the maid exited from the living room.

"The people of color that I know…"

"People of color. How exotic." Mrs. Whitting followed Anita into the kitchen.

"Well, it was us white folks that did start calling them coloreds."

"Oh, Brody, please. You bleeding hearts are all alike."

"I remember some winters that if it weren't for those bleeding hearts we wouldn't have had any shoes or blankets."

"You can't compare what we went through with what the minorities are experiencing now. That's ridiculous." Mrs. Whitting opened the refrigerator and counted trays.

"How?"

"How what?"

"How is it ridiculous? What's so different?"

"Lots of ways." She arched her eyebrows and Anita scooted from the dishwasher to stand next to Mrs. Whitting in front of the refrigerator.

"Well, let's see, you worked your fingers to the bone from secretary, to office manager, to associate assistant, to supervisor, and was just on your way to a top-floor executive office when you met the rich Doctor Whitting and abandoned your career."

"Right. I worked." Mrs. Whitting pointed at the fruit bowl and held up two fingers.

"Not in the fields."

"Exactly."

Anita squatted near the lower shelf of the refrigerator. She cradled one dish in an arm and another on her lap while, with her free hand, she held the second bowl of fruit up in the air for inspection.

"I remember a few summers that you and I..."

"Brody, please." Mrs. Whitting nodded.

"That's the point, Lyna Lou."

"Harriet."

"They're the same as us."

"I worked."

"Yeah, because they were more willing to give the job to poor white trash rather than to a person of color."

Mrs. Whitting had taken a step and stopped.

Silence.

"Lyna Lou, you there?"

Anita could not get up without bumping Mrs. Whitting. She stayed as she was, her arms cramping.

Quiet.

"Harriet?"

"Never use those words with me."

"Why? Because it offends your high-society nose? What would your high falutin' friends say if they knew you grew up in a shack? That you and I stole a roll of tar paper to cover the roof one spring because we were getting rained on?"

Mrs. Whitting walked into the foyer and Anita slumped to the floor, put the bowls down and rubbed her calves.

"Brody, you're overstepping your limits here."

"Maybe, sweet sister, you're understepping yours."

"How? I am not making excuses for them."

"When is Debbie doing the competition? I'll get some time off and drive over and cheer for her."

"Uh, Brody, well, I'm not sure exactly when..."

"Lyna Lou, I've made my point."

"It's not that I'm ashamed of you. Really."

"What else can you call it?"

"It's not what you think."

"Damn." She heard him slap the side of his head. "I'm the one with the law degree and I'm slow. No one there knows where you come from."

"Uh."

"Oh. No one knows about me?"

"Of course, they know I have a brother and that you're a lawyer." From the living room, she looked out the French doors at the tables covered with white linen out on the terrace.

"But not the part that I work non-profit in the barrio."

"Brody, you can be so aggravating."

"Uh huh, she's changed the subject so that can only mean one thing. There's something else. Let me see. Oh, man. I don't believe it. Where have you told them I live?"

"In New York."

"What? I couldn't hear you?"

"In New York. There, are you satisfied?"

Silence.

"Brody, you just don't understand..."

"Understand? As in you're ashamed of your own family. As in you're embarrassed by your own roots. As in you haven't spoken with your mother...in how long?"

"Yes. Yes, I am, but I wouldn't use those exact words. These people would never accept me as their own if they knew how I grew up. They wouldn't romanticize the poverty we grew up in. Not like you and your bleeding heart friends do."

"And *Mamá*?"

"I have nothing to say."

"You usually don't."

"What does that mean?"

"No, I refuse to spell it out and let you off the hook."

"Listen, Brody, *Mamá* wouldn't fit into my life now."

"I'm certain she wouldn't. All those high-society friends of yours wouldn't have one clue as to how to relate to *Mamá* except as a cleaning lady."

"That's unfair."

"But true."

She was quiet. Her breath carried over the line. "There were so many men. She could never hang onto one for very long."

"Yeah, that sucked. But it was also a sign of the times."

"What?"

"At the time, it wasn't right for a woman to live alone like they do now. Having a man in the house made it easier for all of us financially."

"The cost was too high."

"True. Some of the ones she picked weren't up there for the father-of-the-year award, but that's no reason not to see your own ma."

"Brody, you've never called our mother ma. You only do that when you're trying to appear uneducated."

"Caught me."

Mrs. Whitting could practically hear the grin on her brother's face. "And you dare accuse me of trying to pretend I'm something I'm not."

"Lyna Lou..."

"Harriet."

"Yeah. How come you won't talk with her? There has to be more to it than just your high-society friends."

Mrs. Whitting was back in her office. She looked out through the French doors onto the rose garden and saw another yard—packed dirt, a bare, thorny rose bush with no buds, a herd of noisy small children playing with rocks and sticks.

Over the line Brody's voice crowded the picture she was remembering. "I've got an idea of what happened."

The "house" had been a three-room shanty, too hot in the summer and too cold in the winter.

His voice changed. "But I wanted you to tell me."

She and her brother had dragged from the dump an old plaid sofa with maple arms which had sagged in the middle of the front room.

"I've waited for you to tell me."

And the smell. That had been the worst. Fried grease. Lye soap. Dirt washed off, but the smell had stayed in her nose forever.

Mrs. Whitting licked her lips. "It was right after graduation. I was getting ready to go to work. You know how hard it was to get any privacy in that place." Mrs. Whitting guessed her brother was nodding his head. "Stepfather number five was between jobs. He came into the bedroom." She gulped for air to fill the lungs that were compressing with fear. "He tried to kiss me."

"Sis, I'm sorry. You never said..."

"But I did."

"Who'd you tell?" The pitch of the wire hum grew higher, then settled down to a low hum again. "Oh. What did mom say? Did she accuse you of lying?"

"No. At least not that. But..." Mrs. Whitting brushed the tears from her face with the back of her hand. "She said since I was moving out anyway there'd be no reason to start something." A sob slipped across the line.

"That's why you left a month earlier than planned?"

"Uh huh. I had to sleep on the floor of the preacher's house, but it was worth it."

"You told our uncle?"

"Yes, but I had to tell Billie Ray. I had to do something to keep the little ones safe."

"No, you did good. I remember the fight that our uncle had with him. Our stepfather left shortly after you did."

"He came to see me in San Antone."

"He did? I never heard about that."

"He found me working for the church and told the preacher I was some kind of sinner. Accused me right to my face." Harriet pressed her face against the cool pane of glass.

"I wish I had known. I would have knocked him clear over the other county. What came of it?"

"I told the preacher the truth. He believed me and told the man to either stay and cleanse his soul or take his soiled presence away from God."

"That's good. The right thing to do. But why won't you see mom now?"

"It'll take some time before I can forget that she didn't protect me, that she picked him over me." She gulped. "I'm sorry, Brody. I just don't have the kind of forgiving heart you do."

"It's understandable. Just don't take too long, Lyna Lou. Ma's not getting any younger. Living with those types took a toll on her, too."

"So I should forgive her because she couldn't..."

"Whoa. I'm not saying anything. She was a victim just as much as you were. Victims are not good at protecting themselves, much less at teaching their children to protect themselves. Just like, I'm sure, you're teaching your girls how to stand up for themselves now."

"You can bet on that. That's why this Mexican girl is not going to get away with stealing first place from my Debbie. I'll run her into the dirt she came from before I let her hurt my daughter."

"Sis, you may be going to the extreme."

"Never. My daughters are going to know without a doubt that I'm on their side."

"I'm sure they know that already. But sacrificing that poor little girl is not the way to teach them how to stand up for themselves."

"Brody, you just don't understand the situation. I'm here. I see how they act. Don't you trust me to know what I see?"

There was a hesitation on the line. "Of course, I do. It's just that sometimes our histories tend to cloud our view of certain situations."

"I can reassure you that I'm definitely not doing that in these circumstances. My intentions address the issues directly."

Anita stepped into the library.

"Plus when it comes to dealing with minorities, I have a much more subjective attitude than you do. I deal with them as people, not as some downtrodden mass in need of special handouts." Harriet spotted Anita and covered the phone.

Anita reported, "Mrs. Thatcher will be here in a half an hour."

Harriet waved the girl away. "Brody, I've enjoyed talking with you, as always. But I have a luncheon that will be getting under way in less than an hour. I have to go, little brother."

"Don't forget, Lyna Lou, you've been looking up to my six-three since we were thirteen years old."

Harriet laughed and said, "It's Harriet."

"Always remember, when you're standing among all those high-society dames, I love you, Lyna Lou."

"And I love you, Brody." They hung up. Harriet handed the portable phone to Anita as she walked upstairs. "When she arrives, escort Mrs. Thatcher into the den. I'll change and be down."

Anita watched Mrs. Whitting slip into her bedroom to change for the third time that day. That woman had more outfits then Anita's whole family would own in a year.

Several hours later, amid all the society ladies that were attending the prestigious luncheon, Mrs. Harriet Whitting listened attentively as one woman recounted the adventures of her trip abroad. "We had to change planes in this quaint airport. I didn't mind, except for all those raggedy kids let loose. Someone should do something with them. It just wasn't right."

Another woman added, "I know just what you mean. My husband and I were traveling to Houston just last week. Well, the trucks we passed had whole families packed in the back. One of those children could fall off and been crushed by a car before their parents would know."

Anita offered them a tray of hors d'oeuvres.

The woman who had traveled said, "You know, with as many children as those people have, they probably wouldn't even notice if one was missing."

A woman with short brown hair said, "All I can say is I'm glad they love to do stoop labor."

"I heard they have an extra disk in their spine that enables them to do the work in the fields."

Harriet laughed. "Oh that isn't true and you know it. You're just teasing us."

"Harriet, you're such an innocent. You wouldn't know what to do if you found yourself living like they do."

"That's right, Harriet," said the woman with short brown hair. "I can't imagine you in anything less than the best this life has to offer. You were born to this life. Anyone with a fine eye can see that."

Harriet lowered her eyes, sipped from her china cup and smiled.

As Anita stepped away, she watched her employer and smiled, too.

Toasted Too Dark

I hate math. It's just about numbers. They do what they're told to do. Nothing else. How boring.

My parents were very pleased that I liked my computer and spent so much time working on it. Each time they saw me on the computer, they'd smile and say to their friends, "It's put us back a bit, but it was worth it because Justina has never done as well."

To keep them happy, I didn't tell them. I developed a program where, after I entered the math problems, I hit a key and the computer computed the answers. The week before, I got my first "A" in math. The first "A" in my entire life.

Everything was going really good until the week my older, mostly bossy, sister won the spelling bee. After that, Luz was the only person everyone talked about. Thought about. Big deal.

Then one day she walked in with a couple of her girlfriends. Olga and Ana touched the skirt of the organdy, rose-flowered party dress that two of mom's best friends had given Luz to wear to the competition. They rubbed the material against their cheeks and made all kinds of weird noises.

My mom says that in a few years I'll be just like them. I'd rather be dead.

They talked and giggled, their heads close together. I could see their images reflected on my monitor. It was like watching a goofy movie.

Every relative alive—and I think some dead ones too—was calling to tell Luz how proud they were of her. Even a newspaper reporter called. You'd think, at the rate it was swelling, that Luz's head wouldn't be able to fit in our bedroom. Good. She can go live somewhere else.

While Luz was talking on the phone to another relative, Olga held the dress against her body, swinging the skirt wide and admiring herself in the mirror. "This color won't look good on her at all," said Olga.

Little sisters don't count and are rarely noticed. I held my breath and kept my fingers still.

"Maybe, if they shorten the skirt and cut a bit off around the neck, it would help." Ana pointed at the lacy neckline.

They both laughed as Ana took it and pressed it against her body.

"Oh, it looks good on you. Much better than on Luz." Olga squinted into the mirror.

They laughed together. Ana covered her mouth with one hand. Olga squeezed her waist from laughter. The dress slipped off Ana's body and floated to the floor. They both grabbed for the dress. When it hit the floor, a slight tearing sound filled the room.

Ana and Olga stopped and raised their heads to stare at each other. They checked the garment in their hands and saw the rip in the skirt of the dress. Olga quickly looked over at me; I stuck my face in a math book.

Ana slipped the dress onto the hanger and Olga hooked it on the door. My sister had left the dress hanging there all week, so it would be the first thing she saw each morning and the last thing she saw at night.

The two girls moved away from the dress. Ana thumbed through Luz's homework. "*Hijole*, she's done all the problems for tomorrow's homework."

Olga reached over Ana's arms. "No way. She thinks she's so hot." She snapped the notebook open.

"Hey, what you doing?" Ana stared at her friend.

"I'll make a copy of it tonight. In the morning, we'll tell her we found it on the floor next to her locker."

Ana backed up. "I don't know..."

"She's so wrapped up with that spelling bee thing, she'll never figure it out. You'll see." Olga slipped the page into her notebook and noticed the desk drawer open. She stuck her hand inside of the drawer, and withdrew a candy bar.

"Hey, what if Luz sees you."

Olga shrugged as she walked across the room and dropped the wrapper in my waste basket. "What're you working on?" she asked me.

Ana looked over Olga's shoulder. "Hey, I remember doing those baby problems. They're not anything really hard."

I opened my mouth when Luz rushed in, her hand automatically touching the dress. "You'll never believe who that was on the phone. Ricardo."

An "I-told-you-so" look crossed between Ana and Olga.

The three of them huddled on the Luz's bed with the big César Chávez poster on the wall above it. Luz played Selena on the tape deck really loud and I had to put on my earphone.

A while later, Olga headed to the bathroom. Ana moved next to Luz. "Tomorrow could I come over and you can help me do the homework? I just can't get those algebra problems."

"What time? Doesn't Olga work after school?"

"I mean, just you and me. You're so smart and understand this stuff so much better than Olga. Things are just easier with you."

Luz nodded.

Ana lowered her voice. "Don't tell Olga. Okay?"

Luz cocked her head.

"She's so insecure." Ana's eyes filled with big tears. "Her feelings get hurt too much. You know how she is."

Luz and Ana pitched their voices lower as their heads bumped and they burst out laughing as Olga walked in. "What's so funny?" She looked at her two friends.

Together they answered, "Nothing."

Luz reached into the desk drawer. "I've got this really great candy bar. Want some?"

Olga tossed her hair. "Not me. I have to be careful to keep my figure just right."

Luz didn't hear because she was pulling out the drawer. She dumped the drawer's contents on top of her bed, some of it falling on the floor. "Hey, my candy bar is missing."

Ana looked at her feet. Olga searched among Luz's books on top of the desk. "I wonder who could have taken it." She looked in my direction.

Luz caught the reference, stomped across the room and searched in my waste basket. "What's this doing here?" She stuck the ripped candy wrapper under my nose.

I batted it away with my hand. "Get away from me."

"I told you—mom told you to stay out of my desk."

I raised my voice to match hers. "I never got in your desk."

"Oh!" Luz leaned down over me. "I guess this candy wrapper just walked across the room."

I stood up. "Well, Turd Face, that's just what happened."

Luz moved around the corner of the desk and stood in front of me. "Yeah, how Hog Breath?"

I took a step toward her. "Ask your friends." I swung my thumb at her two girlfriends who were edging towards the door.

Olga chirped. "We got to get going. See you at school tomorrow. We'll meet at your locker. Okay?"

Ana waved a limp hand in our direction.

Luz thrust herself against me.

I stood where I was.

She was adding up all the stupid things I had done this past week. "You're just jealous."

"Of what? You got nothing I want." I had been jealous. I had gotten tired of hearing about her success.

"Then how come this." She stuck the candy wrapper under my nose again, impatience winning over sisterly love.

I snatched the wrapper out of her hand and threw it across the room. "Who cares."

"*Mamá* will, when I tell her you were in my desk again."

"You've got worse problems."

"What you mean?"

"Check out your homework."

Luz stared at me, trying to decide if I was distracting her from what I had done. Shaking her head, she walked across the room and opened her notebook. She flipped a few pages in each direction. When she couldn't find her homework, she looked up at me. "You took my homework too."

I whirled around and shouldered my face in front of hers. "You wish."

We stared at each other, taking short, quick breaths onto the fuse of our anger. Our eyes blazed. Muscles knotted down my spine. The hair on the back of my neck rose in anticipation. We circled each other like two cock roosters, stalking a weak spot to attack.

She always blames me for everything. Luz's face was flushed with sweat on her upper lip.

I squinted my eyes to keep the fear from showing. Luz wanted to be a winner. In everything.

As we stepped around each other, Luz tripped over the junk from the desk drawer and stumbled forward. She slammed against my shoulder, pitching me backward. We grabbed at each other, gripping arms, twisting and turning to stay standing.

We regained our footing to stare in shock, hands on each other's arms. "You hit me!" I cried out.

"You hurt my arm!" came back Luz.

We drew back, releasing our hands, startled at the potential of hurting each other. "You hit me first!" I said, taking another step back from disaster.

Luz stepped backwards and flipped the chair over, almost falling. The loud crash filled the room.

My shoulder was sore. I felt the anger jam my throat. Luz was rubbing the back of her leg. We had hurt each other. Fear slid by the anger, and I tasted it.

She stared at me and I stared at her. Luz rubbed her forehead. "You hurt?" I shook my head. She spun around and fixed her dress on the doorway.

I held my breath, thinking she would blame me if she found the rip. But just then my mother walked in. "Luz, I have to talk with you." My mother had been crying.

"What's wrong?"

My mother sat on the edge of Luz's bed. Luz sat next to her. I moved over and dropped on my bed, the cover billowing around me. It was then that my mother noticed the mess in the room.

"What's going on here?" As Luz opened her mouth, *Mamá* said, "Don't tell me nothing. You two been fighting?"

Luz hung her head and nodded.

My mother called me. "Come here."

"I'm sleepy, *Mamá*," I said, hoping she would leave me alone.

"Justina, get over here."

I responded to my mother's tone more than to her words. With a long sigh, I dragged myself over and sat down next to her.

She looked from me to my sister. "Which one of you is going to tell me?"

Both of us looked away.

"Luz?"

"Ask her. She started it."

My mother shifted around on the bed to peer into my face. "Justina, talk to me."

"It's nothing."

"*Mira hija*, I want to know."

I looked up and it seemed like my mother was about to cry. "Don't cry, *Mamá*. I didn't mean it."

She waited.

I sighed. "Luz accused me of going into her desk."

"And?"

Somehow she always knew there was more. "And it wasn't me."

Luz jumped in. "Who else could it have been?"

I hung my head down and twisted the bedspread around my fingers. *Mamá* looked up into my face. My shoulders slumped forward. "It was Olga that took it."

Luz jumped up. "No way. You're making it up."

"Am not. Just wait until tomorrow. She took your homework, too, and she's gonna tell you she found it near your locker."

Luz eyed me as she was deciding how much to believe. "Then why didn't you tell me?"

"You never gave me the chance. Just like you haven't given anyone else the chance for anything ever since you won that spelling contest."

My mom smiled. "I'm sorry *mija*. I know Luz has been a bit overwhelmed with her good fortune. I forgot how hard it could be on little sisters." *Mamá* hugged me.

I shrugged out of her hug. I had a week of stored-up hurts. "But the grown ups are all the time asking about when am I going to do something as good as my sister."

"*Mijita*, I can't defend the insensitivity of some grown ups, but we have always thought you were the best. Each of you, in your own ways, are special to us. That is how it has always been."

"But I get so tired of hearing about her." I pointed at Luz.

"*Mira*, just the other day, we were telling someone about the smart program you made to do your math problems."

I stared at my mother with my mouth open. "You knew?" She nodded. "How?"

"Your father and I talked about it with your teacher and we figured that making that program was harder than solving the problems."

"My teacher knows too?" I just couldn't believe what I was hearing.

"But right now, it is important that we stick together." She turned back to Luz. "That phone call that you just heard..."

Luz nodded. "It was someone wishing me good luck?"

The sound of my mother's voice told me something was very wrong.

"No it wasn't." My mom took my sister's hand. "It was the school principal. He had something very serious to tell us."

Luz moved onto her knees and held her breath. We both knew that our mother would never tell us bad news.

"The school board met the other night. They had this long talk..."

Luz gulped. "About me?"

Mamá nodded. "Someone told them that you stole the list of the words used at the spelling bee."

Luz jumped to her feet. "They saying I stole the words to the contest?"

"Mrs. Cuellar has arranged for them to hold an open school meeting in two days." *Mamá* reached out and touched my sister's arm. "They said they are willing to listen to whatever we have to say, but..." *Mamá* shrugged.

"But I do know the spelling. I do. I won fair and square." Luz stomped her foot. "You know I did, *Mamá*. You know it. Tell them."

"I did, *Mijita*. I told them over and over. But they insisted that measures had to be taken to set a good example for the future."

I could tell that mom was hurting as bad as Luz was.

"That means..." Luz stomped across the room, swooped the dress off the door, and threw it across the room. Like a ghost of a dream, the dress fluttered to a crumpled heap on the floor. "I don't care. They can take their spelling bee, for all I care. I didn't want to go anyway." Luz held her head high. I could see that her chin was quivering.

I picked up the dress. Smoothing out the wrinkles, I hung the dress back up on the door, then stood in front of my sister. "I care. You would have beaten them all."

Luz collapsed into *Mamá's* arms, crying. I sat on the other side of my sister, rubbing her back. Luz reached out and took my hand.

"You would have won. I know you would have," I said softly.

Luz opened her eyes and stared past our mother.

"Honest." I crossed my heart.

"You really think so?" Luz looked at me.

"Yup. No one can beat you in spelling."

"There's a part, inside of me, that was kinda of scared that maybe I would lose." Luz said it so softly that I had to lean over to hear.

Mamá stroked her hair. "*Mijita...*"

I said first, "No way. You're better than the electronic dictionary everyone gave you last week. You don't take no batteries." I giggled as Luz grinned through her tears. "You know, whenever I'm writing a paper, it's you that fixes my spelling. You would have won. I'm totally sure of that. So are you. That's why your head got so big."

Luz sat up and stuck her finger in my face. *Mamá* raised a hand. I grinned. Luz stopped and smiled back.

"You had a right to feel like the best. You are the best." I hugged my sister.

"You're still a Hog Breath."

"Turd Face."

We giggled into each other' shoulders.

The next morning, I waited until Luz left. Then I whispered to my *abuelita* about the rip in Luz's dress. As I left for school, I saw my *abuelita* sitting in the front room with her sewing box out and Luz's dress on her lap. I smiled. Luz would never find out.

Little sisters are good to have around, sometimes.

Bleached Wheat

My mom smiles a lot. People are always saying, "Sally Jane, you have such a happy mom." At home, alone, it's different.

My mom has a wall in her bedroom lined with sixties' videos. Beach Party Movies. Gidget movies. Sweet-innocent-girls-always-win movies. Sweet innocent blonde girls, that is. I always rooted for dark-haired Annette to win.

Every weekend when I was younger, my mom would make a big bowl of popcorn and buy several liter-bottles of Big Red soda, and we would watch two or three videos. Mom would point out the way good girls acted.

Now, when she gets on that kick again, I just sit there, arms folded, a bored look on my face. These videos from the sixties don't have anything in them that's me or about my life, so why waste my time? But then I went and saw *Mi Vida Loca*—a movie about Chicana homegirls. I knew nothing about their lives either. So where does that leave me?

Sitting in front of the dresser, with make-up lights surrounding the mirror, I brush my hair back into a ponytail like the girls in the video wear their hair. My mom wants me to wear it that way. If I don't, she'll comb my hair. She yanks and pulls when she does my hair, so I'd rather do it myself.

I pick up the phone on the second ring. Sofia sounds breathless on the other end. "My mom's gonna be gone for awhile. What if I come over and we can do our math homework together?"

She's sweet. She knows I can't add two plus two, but she'd never say so. "Sure."

I run into the kitchen. My mom's busy making food for the church bake sale after Mass tomorrow. I take a deep breath, filling my nose with the smells of cupcakes and brownies. My mom has dried cookie dough on the side of her arm. She's not much taller than I am, and she lightens her short brown hair. She says she's not bleaching it. But each time she washes her hair, it gets lighter and sticks out like a broom. It looks weird because her eyebrows are darker.

"Mom, Sofia's coming over." She slaps my hand away as I reach for a cookie.

"Again? Wasn't she just here yesterday?"

"So?"

"So? So? Is that all you can think of to say?"

"I guess."

"Guess? Guess? You have to sound confident. People will never put their trust in you if you don't sound confident."

My mom is always saying stuff like that. I haven't been able to figure out why she thinks I want people to put their trust in me. "So?"

"I hope you don't talk to your teachers like that. You have to think about getting into college and they're the ones who are going to write your letters of recommendation. You have to impress them now for what you want later."

This is something else I hear a lot but don't understand. Most times my teachers talk to me about secretarial courses or factory work. I believe I am going to college more than they do. "So?"

My mother waves the spatula in the air. I dodge a splatter of cookie dough. "Doesn't Sofia have any place else to go?"

"She wants to help me with..."

"You're so gullible. In time you'll understand that these girls are not your friends. They're jealous of you and like hanging out with you because of all the pretty things you have."

Gripping the door tightly, I open the refrigerator and grab a soda. I yank the pop-up and the soda fizzles and spills onto the floor. I leave it there until my mother coughs and I grab a towel and clean it up.

"Sofia's coming over to help me with my homework because I'm so stupid about math." There, I said it. See if she can make anything out of that.

"Sofia's a nice girl, but she's so dark. You have to start thinking about those kinds of things. You're going to go far. On to college. Probably get a Ph.D. in something major. Only five percent of people with Ph.D.'s are Latinos. And you have to know that most of that five percent are men."

Yes, I know that. It is burned in my brain along with all the other sayings she repeats to me each day. My mother wants me to do well in this world. It makes me feel good that she believes I can. But sometimes, I get scared that I'm going to disappoint her. "Sofia's been my friend for a long time."

"For when you were a child, that was nice. Now you have to think of your future. People as dark as Sofia are a hindrance. God made light-skinned people so we could get ahead in the world."

Sometimes I wonder if I did disappoint my mom, would she still love me? "Sofia is smarter than me in school."

"You don't see the teachers praising her at open house, no? I'm sure she will do very fine for her type of people. I don't hold anything against Sofia. It must be hard with a mother like Manela. I went to grade school with her. She was trouble then and now. She is always mouthing off about something at the PTA meetings. Rocking the boat only makes people believe we're all troublemakers. That's why you need to think about who you're seen with and important stuff like that.

"The whites rule this world. To get ahead in it, you have to play by their rules. People like poor Sofia, who are so dark, don't have a chance." My mother is shaking her head in sympathy as she pulls out another tray of cookies from the oven.

I hear a soft cough and turn around. Sofia is standing just outside the screen door; her clothes make a bright spot of color.

"I like her, but it's just so sad that with a mother like..."

"Mom, look who's here already," I say loudly as I jump up to hold the screen door open for Sofia.

My mother looks up and smiles. I can see her judging the embroidered smock tucked into a gathered, multi-colored skirt that Sofia is wearing. "Ah, see how nice you look in that outfit. Just like what the old women wear in Mexico. Very traditional. Is this something your mother thought of?"

Sofia takes the soda I hand her. "No ma'am. My grandmother gave it to me. It was what she wore when she visited the President in Mexico."

We race to my bedroom.

On my canopy bed, the style straight out of a Sandra Dee movie, we lay flat on our backs, our butts against the headboard, our feet on the wall. Ruffled toss pillows share the bed with stuffed teddy bears, pandas and a giraffe. None of them have names. They're my mother's additions. They're identical to the ones the stars in the videos had on their beds.

On a shelf on either side of the bed stand dolls all in a row. Collector dolls, dressed in satin and lace from all over the world. All pink skin and blonde hair. I wish I could hide them, but Sofia's already seen them. She says they don't bother her.

I ask, "You want to hear some music?"

"What you got?"

"I got the New Kids on the Block tape yesterday."

"*Hijo*, they're so pansy. All the white girls think they're so cute." She sticks her finger in her mouth, and pretends to gag. "You got any Dr. Loco's Rockin' Jalapeño Band tapes?"

I nod and search through the piles of tapes on the shelf. Behind me, I hear her ask, "How come your mother doesn't like me?"

I sit back on the bed and we are each squeezing a stuffed animal. "She likes you. A lot. It's just that she wants me to go far. She's got lots of plans for me."

"My mom makes plans for me too. Do you ever think..."

"If I can be what she wants?" I look at Sofia, hoping she has an answer. "I think about it all the time."

Sofia sighs. "Do you want to do your homework?"

"I guess." Neither of us moves. We bat the stuffed toys in the air. "Have you ever thought about what you're going to do after high school?" I hold on to my stuffed critter and wait for a response.

"College, probably. Except we probably won't have the money to send both me and my brother. My mom is really furious that my brother is going and I'm not. She's looking for another job to get the money for me." Sofia sighs. "Nothing comes easy." She turns on her side and rests her head on her hand. "Is being lighter really nicer?"

"Why're you asking me?"

"Because you are the lightest of Justina, Diana, me and you."

"You heard my mom, didn't you?"

Sofia shakes her head. "Nope."

I know she is being agreeable. Not the kind my mom means, but the thoughtful kind that makes good girlfriends. "Sometimes, I guess. I get help at department stores without too much hassle."

Both of us remember the time that Sofia was followed by security the whole time she was in the store.

I say, "The teachers don't raz on me like they do the others."

Sofia nods. She always sits in the back of the room.

"But they expect more. I'm always hearing that I have to live up to my potential. I've got much more to prove."

Sofia lies back down, and tosses the animal she's holding into the air over to me. "Sounds hard in a different way. No one expects anything from me and when I do good, they wonder if I cheated."

I bat the panda over to her, keeping it in the air. "It's so unfair. You're smarter than me most times."

She catches the stuffed panda and hits me on the head, laughing. "We're both smart, just in different ways."

I grab a teddy bear and swing back. She hits me back and soon, we are slugging it out. We're standing on the bed, laughing so hard we keep missing each other. When we get tired of swinging, we collapse back on to the bed, sitting cross-legged, facing each other. After we catch our breath, I ask her, "What's it like being so beautiful?"

Sofia blushes, her dark skin tinged with the kind of red you see in a sunset. "I'm not beautiful."

"Baloney. When we walk down the hallway at school, all the boys do is stare at you. I heard one say that you're so beautiful, he's afraid to talk to you."

Sofia bows her head. I look at her for a moment.

"Oh. That's the hard part," I say, getting the idea.

Sofia nods. "Most people think I am either stuck up or stupid because of how I look. I don't see how I'm so different than any one of you."

"Cheez! Sofia just look in the mirror." Her long black hair, the color of lava, flows down her back.

"But I don't want to be beautiful if it's going to make it hard for other people to talk with me."

"Maybe so. But it seems to me that God saved all the special parts just to make you. Can I touch your face?"

Sofia drew back. "*¿Por qué?*"

"I don't know. Because your face is like those paintings we see when we go to the museum." I put my thumbs together with my hands spread out like a picture frame and squint through the opening at her face. "Maybe so I can tell myself that you're just like me."

We stare at each other for a moment, then she smiles. "Sure." She leans forward, sticking out her tongue and crossing her eyes.

With both my hands, I touch her dark skin, stretched across broad cheekbones. She feels like smooth, polished mahogany, throbbing with hidden energy. I put one finger on each eyebrow and follow the perfect arch of her dark brows and run the back of my fingers across her fan-like, curly eyelashes. Her nose is thin and I trace her full lips with my fingertip, making a full circle around her mouth. Even the groove between her mouth and her chin feels warm and soft. I run a fingertip down one side of her jaw and up the other side. I drop my hands and stare at her eyes, a mixture of brown and gold that flicker like a satin dress.

She laughs. "Am I real?"

I can tell she's uncomfortable with my inspection, so I sniff and say, "Except you smell so much like rice and beans."

She jumps on me and we tumble to the floor, wrestling.

"Take it back."

"No I won't." We roll across the floor.

From the end of the hallway, I hear, "Are you girls doing your homework?"

We answer in harmony. "Yes ma'am."

We giggle as we pull our books down onto the floor with us.

A couple of hours later, we are in the kitchen eating cookies. The phone rings and I answer it. "Mom, it's Mrs. Thatcher. For you," I yell down the hallway.

My mom jets out of the bathroom and scowls at me. She mouths the words, "Don't yell into the phone." She rushes into her bedroom and picks up the phone. I hear, "Emily, how thoughtful of you to call." I hang up the extension in the kitchen.

Sofia nods at the phone. "Isn't that Tiffany's mother?"

"Yeah." I stuff another cookie into my mouth.

"I didn't know you knew her." Sofia pushes the plate of cookies away.

"I don't. Mom does volunteer work with her mother."

Sofia puts her glass in the sink. "I better get home."

"But didn't you say your mom was out all afternoon?"

"Yeah, but I don't want to be here if Tiffany's coming over."

I stand up. "Why you acting *pendeja*? I told you, I don't hang with Tiffany."

Sofia hangs her head, looking at the floor as she swings one foot in a semi-circle in front of her.

"When have you ever seen her talk to me at school?"

Sofia brightens. "We better get to the rest of the homework before everybody finds out how dumb you really are."

"You're saving my butt, *amiga*." We slap palms in the air and go down the hallway.

My mom pops out of her bedroom. "*Mija*, get something nice on. Tiffany and her mother are coming over. We're going to work on letters petitioning the school board to give Luz Ríos another chance."

She is zipping up a pink knit dress she usually wears to church.

Sofia bobs her head. "Oh yeah, my mom's gonna do something too. Luz never would've cheated. Can I help lick envelopes or something?"

"Sofia, I'm sorry, you'll have to go home now. Maybe you can help your mother with whatever she's doing. I can imagine it's quite interesting." She points at me, "Put on that ruffled green dress I got you last week. I want you looking proper."

Sofia sits on my bed and watches me dress. I change the ribbon on my ponytail to match the green dress. "*Hijo*, I hate this. I absolutely hate having to wear this outfit on a Saturday when this is my day to hang out in jeans. I don't know why I have to do this."

My mother sticks her head in the door. "Be sure to put on your black, patent-leather pumps."

I roll my eyes to Sofia. "Yes, ma'am."

Sofia is packing her books into her knapsack.

"Hey, you not talking to me?"

Sofia turns around, tossing her knapsack over her shoulder. "I thought you said you didn't know Tiffany."

"I don't. This is my mother's idea. Remember?"

Sofia heads toward the door.

I grab her by the arm. "Hey, I can't help it if my mom's all stupid when it comes to white people."

Sofia laughs. "You shouldn't talk about your mom like that."

"Yeah, but it's true. Now we can't spend the rest of the day together."

My mother comes in. "Oh, Sofia, you're still here. You are leaving?"

"Mom. Please."

"Yes, ma'am. I'm going."

From my bedroom window, I wave to Sofia as she reaches the curb. She doesn't wave back. She commands all the space around her, her head high, her black hair flowing behind her like a cloak. For a moment, with the sun beating down on her head and the bright light reflecting off her clothes, she reminds me of the pictures I saw of Aztec women, regal and majestic. I watch as she disappears down the street.

As I open the door to let them in, I groan. Tiffany has on a lime-green T-shirt, jeans and sneakers with fluorescent green laces. Her blond hair hangs loose around her shoulders. She takes in my outfit and lifts her blue eyes to her mother.

Mrs. Thatcher smiles. "Is your mother home?"

I swallow my giggle. Mrs. Thatcher has on a yellow jumper with a saffron-colored blouse that pinches shut at her neck. Her lemon-colored hair shags down past her shoulders. But the black oxfords reveal the preacher's wife.

My mom comes into the foyer, wiping her hands on a kitchen towel. "Emily, it's so good to see you. I'm glad you thought of asking me to help." Mom shepherds us into the kitchen. "I was thinking we could set up the girls here in the kitchen with a typewriter. One of them could stamp the return address and the other could type in people's addresses."

"Sounds like an excellent idea. You're always so organized, Helen." Mrs. Thatcher smiles, a you're-a-good-child-of-God smile.

"You and I can work on the letter on my computer in the den." Mom points down the hallway.

Mrs. Thatcher puts her hand to her throat. "Oh, you understand all that technological stuff. Computers just leave me baffled."

Mom laughs softly. "Oh Emily, I'm sure you're underestimating your talents." Switching to us, she dictates, "You two stay in Sally Jane's bedroom until we have everything in order."

I can't think of a thing to talk about to Tiffany and I'm worried that Sofia won't understand why I had to do this. Unsure of what to say, I don't say anything.

In my bedroom, Tiffany walks around the room, looking at and touching everything. She lifts the music box sitting on the dresser with the ballerina on top that spins and puts it back in a different place. She stops at the closet and stares. She swings her head around, seeing the soft, under-the-panel light-ing, the ceiling painted a robin's-egg blue, the trim an off-white. A beige, textured carpet blankets the floor. Mirrors camouflage the sliding doors on both sides of the room. When she walks in, she has a reflection of the reflection of herself.

"Gosh, I didn't know y'all lived this well off."

I don't say anything. I can't. For sure, my mom would really be mad at me.

Tiffany straightens the comforter, then sits beside me on the bed. "Can I ask you something?"

Uh, oh, I think. Whenever they start a question like that, it means bad news. "What?"

"How does it feel to work in the fields all the time?"

I hang onto the bedpost tight. "Tiffany, I've never worked in any fields my whole life."

"Really?" She looks at me surprised. "My mom says it's nothing to be ashamed of."

I stare back at her.

"Well, then how is it having your parents work in the fields?"

I think about all the time my mom donates to the charities that Tiffany's mother sponsors. I guess their idea of charity is different. "Look, me and my family have never worked in the fields. I don't even know anyone who does or has ever worked in the fields."

"Really! That's so amazing."

Before I let go of the bedpost and get myself into real trouble, I ask, "What do you want to do?"

She spies the tape I had shown Sofia on top of my stereo cabinet. "Oh, you've got the new Kids On the Block tape. I just think they're so max. The lead singer is so totally cute. Makes my heart just go." She flaps her hand over the area of her heart.

I laugh really hard, then swallow it down when she looks at me funny.

My mom comes into the room. "Everything's ready. Come on into the kitchen."

We trail behind her with about as much enthusiasm as if we are going to a funeral. The typewriter is sitting on the kitchen table and about a trillion envelopes are stacked high against the wall on the table.

"You," she points at me, "can stamp the envelopes with the return address. Tiffany can type the address from this list." She holds up a sheaf of paper an inch thick.

Tiffany and I trade looks that tell each other what we think of grown-ups.

"How come Tiffany gets to do the typing?"

I could tell by the look on my mother's face that I had set myself up for a lecture. "Because she is using her education to prepare herself for a better future. Typing is the next step to computers."

I give a loud, martyred sigh as my mom leaves the room.

After a half an hour, my mom and Mrs. Thatcher return with the letter all ready. "While Emily takes the letter to be copied and runs to the post office to buy postage, I thought you girls would enjoy watching a video."

"Yeah, that'd be great." Anything to keep me from being alone with Tiffany.

"Video?"

I nod, vigorously. "They're beach party movies. They're loads of fun."

"You mean the ones with Sandra Dee and Bobby Darin?"

"Yeah. They're great. C'mon. Let's watch them." I signal her to follow me out into the living room. She follows.

After my mom waves Mrs. Thatcher off, she comes in carrying platters of brownies and cookies, the ones she cooked for the church bake sale, the ones she wouldn't let me and Sofia touch. "I thought you would want something to drink." She hands Tiffany a Dr. Pepper and looks at me with a Dr. Pepper in her other hand.

I stare. She's been forcing us to drink the grocery brand of soda for so long, I started to like the taste of it. Now she's handing Tiffany a Dr. Pepper and she wants me to drink one too. "I'm not thirsty."

"Oh, we're going to be a poop today. Well, Tiffany and I can enjoy ourselves just as well." Mom punches the remote.

The credits fill the screen with all that funky music that goes with these movies. I slump into the corner of the sofa, putting my feet on the coffee table.

"Honey," my mother's voice drips with saccharin, "you know that's not allowed."

I let my feet drop to the floor with a thud.

If someone told me, I never would have believed it. I would tell them that they lied. But sure enough, Tiffany and my mother are watching this movie and laughing together. Except my mother is laughing with

Tiffany at all the parts that my mother had told me are clear examples of stupidity. She is laughing at all the actions she told me never, never to do.

The doorbell rings. We are at the part when the black-haired girl's jealousy against the blonde girl is exposed.

My mom looks at the door with disgust, then at me. I ignore her, but she looks harder and motions with her head for me to go get the door.

I open the door to find Mrs. Thatcher standing there; her hands are full of boxes. "Mom," I yell, "it's Mrs. Thatcher."

My mom springs into the foyer. "Honey, you know we don't yell like that in this household." She frowns at me while turning her head to smile at the woman walking in. "Emily, how did it go? Were you able to get everything?" She relieves Mrs. Thatcher of the boxes in her arms and sets them on the table near the door. "Your daughter and I were just having a wonderful time, weren't we, Tiffany?"

Tiffany has walked into the foyer to stand with all of us. "We're watching a really old movie. It's pretty dumb."

Mrs. Thatcher smiles over her head at my mother. "Tiffany, that's not polite to say." She reaches inside of her handbag. "Here is all the postage. I'm truly sorry, but I completely forgot. I have another meeting I just have to attend. I can't stay any longer."

My mother's face changes from unhappy to happy in a matter of a shift that only this daughter can see. "Of course, I understand. If you have some time later maybe you could come by and help me finish stuffing these envelopes."

Mrs. Thatcher nods. "I'll try. But I know what a reliable, hard worker you are, and I'm sure that it will all be in the mail by tonight. The special PTA meeting is the day after tomorrow, so the letters have to get out quickly." She smiles an I'm-so-proud-of-you smile.

Mrs. Thatcher guides Tiffany by the shoulders to stand in front of her, facing us. "Tiffany, tell Mrs. Mendoza 'thank you' and that you had a marvelous time."

Tiffany's lips respond to the command. "Thank you, Mrs. Mendoza. I had a delightful time."

Mrs. Thatcher squeezes Tiffany's shoulders.

"Thanks, Sally Jane. I'll see you in school Monday."

Her bubbly words say something different from what I see in her eyes. I know not to mention to anyone at school, in her group or mine, that she spent time here. I don't say anything.

My mom kicks me on the heel of my shoe.

"Sure, Tiffany. See you Monday," I say with my Sandra Dee smile.

As Mom follows them out the door, she delivers an expression over her shoulder that, as her veteran daughter, I know means no milk and cookies for me tonight. She walks them to their car. "Drive carefully." My mom waves at the disappearing car.

From the doorway, I see Tiffany slump down in the front passenger seat. Mrs. Thatcher turns toward her daughter. Her head bobs once or twice. A moment later, Tiffany sits up. I smile. Tiffany just received the "sit-up-straight-or-you'll-grow-up-with-a-crooked-back" lecture. I guess there are some things that are the same no matter what culture you grow up in.

In the kitchen, my mom is opening the boxes. I grab a brownie. "Put those back. They're for tomorrow at church."

"But mom, you let Tiffany..."

"Put it back. You just don't appreciate what I do for you."

"What do you do for me? You let Tiffany eat these brownies, but I can't. You let Tiffany drink what she wants, but I have to drink store brand. You let Tiffany hang out here, but you send my girlfriend home."

"That's enough. Watch your step or I'll tell your father."

"And Mrs. Thatcher's way too busy to spend any time with you. You don't even get it."

My mother turns on me. "I get it. Don't make any mistake about that. I get it. But I know what I want. I know where we're heading. And someday, you'll see, she'll be wanting to spend time with me. You just wait and see."

She stomps off down the hallway, saying, "You just don't appreciate what you have. The expensive clothes, the Catholic education, all of that. I never had anything like that when I was your age. I made a promise that it would be different for you. You would have chances and opportunities I never had. And maybe, for now, you can't understand enough to appreciate how I have sacrificed for you, but you will. Then maybe you'll realize how much I've done for you." She slams her bedroom door behind her.

I grab a brownie and stuff the whole square into my mouth. I choke, spit it out and throw it into the trash. I slip down the wall and sit on the floor.

I'm not sure I know what my mother wants from me. Sometimes I thinks she wants me to be the best, light-skinned person there is. Except in Tiffany's world, I'll never be light enough. It's with my girl-friends that I feel okay and they let me be just fine. Isn't that what counts?

I reach up and take the phone off the hook and slide back down the wall. I dial and let it ring. "Are you still mad at me?"

"Mad? At what?" Sofia whispers into the phone and I press the receiver closer against my ear.

"Because my mother made you go home. Because of Tiffany." I cross my fingers.

"Nah. I told my mom about it and she said that your mom's been acting like that since they were kids. It's got nothing to do with me."

"We're still friends?" I hold my breath.

"¿Cómo no? Unless that Tiffany bleached all the Mexican out of you."

"No way, man." I eye the boxes on the kitchen table with all the envelopes. "Hey, you get Diana and come over. I'll call Justina. We're going to send out some letters tonight." A grin spreads across my face. "You can do the typing."

Authentic Tortillas

The darkness in San Antonio drops like a blanket over the city after the colorful symphony has crossed the Texas sky. It is a sky so big, you would think that everyone underneath it could live in harmony.

I shift my body trying to get more comfortable in the lawn chair. The webs pinch my back. I sit alone in the backyard of my daughter's home. I change positions again, uncomfortable under the weight of knowledge that my age brings me.

My daughter peers through the night and spots the red tip of my *cigarillo*. I know she sighs at the old woman—black felt reservation hat with the beaded hatband, pulled over low on my forehead, long hair loose down my back and held together at the back of the neck with a leather thong.

Once I braided my hair as a good wife and as a good employee. Now, no more. My vanity has left me nothing but my hair to show off and I love the feel of it on my skin.

From the other side of the house, Luz, my oldest granddaughter, approaches with hair brush in hand. Since her victory at the spelling bee, family and friends have been putting their desires for *la causa*, for *La Raza*, on her shoulders to carry on stage with her.

At fourteen, she is still wearing her baby fat, but womanhood is sneaking out in ways that make her parents worry. She waves the hair brush in the air. I smile and nod. The moonlight on her face shows the growing fullness of her lips and the thick lashes over eyes the same brown as the tequila I drink from my glass. She steps behind me and unties the leather string. She grabs hold of my hair in one hand and brushes the snarls out, working her way from the tips up to my head.

My daughter shakes her head and retreats into the kitchen as I suck on the *cigarillo* held between my lips. My granddaughter leans over my shoulder and breathes in. I slap my shoulder and she jerks away, laughing.

Luz is full of the devil, ready to go out in the world and stamp it with her being. She fills my heart with joy. She yearns for adventure, yet sadness fills the shadows. I know; all mothers know, as we watch out young ones buck heads with the world, that bruises and scrapes are sure to occur. Most of them heal over quickly. Others are remembered forever.

"Tell me a story, *Abuelita*," Luz whispers in my ear as she sweeps the brush through my hair.

"Once when I was a young girl—your mother was little—I worked in a restaurant, making *tortillas*. I was so proud that I had a job. I remember being really proud of the *tortillas* I made."

"You going to teach me how, *Abuelita*?" Luz lengthens her stroke on my hair.

"*Sí, mijita*. I can teach you."

Flour, a pinch of salt, a spoonful of baking powder. The hand disappears under the flour. In a steady rhythm the ingredients are sifted together. White puffs tease the nose, the hand is coated in white.

A scoop of lard is dropped in the middle, squeezed into the flour. Flour bits ooze through the fingers. Fingers move in a repetitive motion, the mind slipping into meditation. Grasping, squeezing, dropping, grasping, squeezing so the muscles on the hand make the veins disappear, kneading the lard into the flour, making the ingredients a crumbly mix.

Grabbing the hanger, I hook my clean uniform on the locker door handle. My co-worker, Carmen, who has just finished her shift, frees herself from the embroidered-uniform blouse and pitches it into her locker.

"Aura, did you see Lucy Ricardo last night? She was in trouble as usual." Carmen chuckles at the memory. "I don't know how that Ricky puts up with her. All the men I know would have given her a good whack against the head by now." Carmen, twenty-six, two years older than me, slips her arms through the sleeves of her leopard-skin blouse.

I join in Carmen's laughter. I hang my blue cotton dress on the hook in the locker, then pull off from a hanger a blouse with delicate stitching across the front. "These outfits are for the birds." I struggle to pull the peasant blouse over my head. "How they expect me to cook with this thing falling off my shoulder all the time is something I can't figure out." I pull my black, waist-length braid out from the back of my blouse.

Carmen laughs. "That's the point." She's jerking on a pair of jeans, with rhinestones up the sides of the legs.

"I'm a mother of seven. Why do they want me in this getup?" I fluff the multi-gathered skirt of different colors on the hanger.

"Be thankful that you're not like the skinny Chicanas with the big *chichis*," Carmen holds her hands in front of her chest as if she is holding watermelons. "Them, they want standing at the front door for the customers to see. Us, we give the food a home style look. We are the *mamásitas* that have cooked for generations. Remember the motto?"

We both recite together, laughing, "Authentic before all else."

Carmen holds up a hand and slips on three rings, then does the same thing with the other hand. "I had my break today. But I think they're expecting some kind of huge party tonight. So take it easy as long as you can."

I *think*? Tell me how I'm supposed to take it easy standing on my feet for eight hours. To Carmen I ask, "Did the boss or his wife come in at all?"

Carmen shakes her head. "Because of the party, they'll probably be coming in tonight."

"*Híjo*. Everybody loves Mexican food."

"And Mercuries is the best place to get it," sings Carmen. "Where you get served authentic Mexican food by blonde waiters."

"This place goes out of its way to make the customer feel like they're in Mexico with the paintings on the walls of the rolling hills with prickly cactus."

I chuckle. "And don't forget the huge black velvet pictures of bull fighters and *vaqueros* just like in my living room."

"*Ay*, me too. What good Mexican home would be without it's velvet picture of Elvis." Carmen fluffs her hair. "What I like the most is that the waiters wear white cotton pants that show their underwear."

"At least the bus boys are Latinos. I guess we could have it worse."

"You been in front of that grill too long, *amiga*. The heat's fried your brains."

I drop the full, gathered skirt over my hips. "Como no. I saw a movie the other day. One of those westerns. You know what I mean, where all the good cowboys are *gringos* and are going to save the poor Mexican farmers. When they ride into town, there's always some fat *mexicana* sitting alongside the road with a dozen little children running around her, making *tortillas* on a hot rock. Don't matter what town or how many times they ride in, she's sitting there cooking those damn *tortillas* with that brood of kids."

Carmen steps into her high heels and says, "Let's hope the boss doesn't see that movie. He'll have us cooking on a hot rock to make the place more authentic." We laugh.

Small portions of warm but not hot water are poured into the bowl with one hand while the other hand continues to mix the ingredients. The knuckles are deep canyons of powdery dough. The hand immerses, squeezing, blending, molding. The *masa* takes shape.

A handful of flour is splashed onto the counter. The *masa* is dumped from the bowl onto the dusted counter. A white glob of soft, elastic dough. Both hands slap, pinch, squeeze, punch, work in unison. The sound of wet *masa* sticking to the counter. Lifted, dropped, and lifted again.

The door to the employee's room opens and a man's head appears. "Everyone decent?"

Carmen swings her valise-size tote bag onto the bench and opens it. "You wish, *cabrón*." Carmen says to me, "Enrique, oh, excuse me, Pancho, the boss-man's ass kisser. They stand him out front like a wooden Indian. See, more proof. Our floor manager is authentic."

From the door, Enrique says, "Too much laughter coming from in here. You should get here early enough to get dressed and be out at the grill by your starting time." He looks at his watch. "Time is money."

Carmen turns to him. "We're not like you. We're not willing to work for nothing just for a pat on the head from the master."

"Just wait." Enrique leaves.

"*¡Pendejo!* Who does he think he's kidding?"

I pull at Carmen's arm. "Take it easy, *Chula*. He can make trouble for you."

"*Ay*, Aura, you're such an innocent. He's already forced me into the supply closet and offered me a deal." She smacks her lips as she freshens her ruby-colored lipstick.

"A deal?" I slip on her white loafers with the cushioned pads inside for the long hours ahead.

"Bed." Carmen shakes her head at the innocent look on my face. "If I go to bed with him, I'll get a raise."

"*¡Ay, Díos mío!*"

"Raise, my ass. He can't even change the menu without calling the owner to check it out first." Carmen snaps the cosmetic bag shut and drops it into her tote bag.

I toss my purse and the hanger into the bottom of my locker and clang the door shut. "*Cuidado.* Just be careful." I twist the padlock dial several times and let it go. Tossing my jet-black, waist-length braid over my shoulder, I straighten my back and stick my chin in the air. "My public awaits me."

Carmen laughs, holds open the door and bows. "At the grill today, presenting *Doña* Morales."

The rolling pin is a smooth, round, wooden piece about a foot long, sanded and oiled. Juices from the *masa* seep into the wood. The *palote* acquires a glossy exterior. Dark from long use. Smoothness comes from the hands gripping, clasping, rolling over the wood in a constant motion for many hours. Incomplete is a wedding shower without the bride-to-be receiving at least three *palotes*. The bride knows the *palote* comes in handy for chasing people around the house.

People are ushered to wooden tables set for four that run alongside the wall. Bright red-and-white-checked tablecloths cover the tables. The patrons sit on straight-back, slatted wooden chairs. Linda Ronstadt sings softly in the background. The salad bar sits behind me, an entryway on either end. People make their own salads from the restaurant side of the food bar and watch me also. With my back to the customers, I stand at a small wooden counter rolling out the *tortillas* and cooking them. The area is visible to the dining room for all to see that the *tortillas* they receive at their tables are fresh and hot off the grill.

A young wife nudges her husband and points. "Oh, look how she does that. She's so efficient."

"Too bad you couldn't learn how to make those pancakes. We could have some at home instead of always having to buy them."

"Oh honey, you know it's in their blood." She smiles and gives me a little wave.

Crew cut hair, in a white shirt and tie, he nods and smiles at me. "Hell-lo," he pronounces slowly.

With a twist that could break the neck of a chicken, a chunk is broken off from the huge lump of dough. The hands knead each chunk, rolling it under, making smooth round patties of dough, *bolitas de masa*, lined up in a row on a long, flat metal tray.

The people that are visible in the pass-through appear as waving images behind the curtain of heat radiating from the three-by-two grill. One ball of *masa* is taken from the tray and placed on the counter.

The hours feel like days; the minutes refuse to pass. I cannot sneeze, scratch my nose, or fix my hair. I'm not even allowed to sweat. I can't move from the counter, and going to the bathroom takes permission from God. My feet itch, and I rub one foot against the back of the other leg, not even getting close to the itch, not stopping the itch, just ruining my hose.

I let the tension slide out through my hands as I continue to roll. The movement of the *palote* in my hand reaches all the way into my back and fills the space that is my body, while my mind filters through the parts that are my real life. I have learned to blank out the people milling through the restaurant, only seeing the small space in front in me. The noise from the restaurant becomes a scratchy old record playing in the background of my thoughts. I list all the chores I have to get done before I might have some time to spend with my sketch book.

The *palote* is rolled over the *masa* in brisk, short snaps of the wrist, going repeatedly first straight, then to the right and then to the left. The *masa* stretches in the direction of the pressure. As the *masa* flattens, the stroke of the rolling pin lengthens.

The arm muscles rolling the *palote* on the *masa* stretch against the skin, forming ridges and hollows.

The strokes pull on the dough as the muscles pull on the arm. Every few strokes, the tortilla is lifted, turned slightly, and dropped back down onto the counter. The *palote* rounds out the edges, stretches the dough, making a perfect circle of food.

The waiters wear white shirts with wide, red sashes wrapped around their waists that hang down the sides of their legs. Often sash tails get caught under a tray or pinched between chairs causing no end to the disarray. The waitresses also wrap their waists with red sashes, the end hanging lower than the gathered skirts they wear. Their peasant blouses, held around the shoulder with a red ribbon, slip at the most crucial times.

"Waiter! Waiter!" A man with a foghorn for a voice yells until a waiter appears at his table. "Here. Give this to the little lady making the tortillas. These are the best damn tortillas I've ever tasted."

I wonder how he would know, since he drank more than he ate. But I smile politely when the waiter drops my tip into a glass on the shelf above my head. The man winks as his elbow slips off the table. I pray that he has gone home long before I get off work.

Domingo, a busboy, steps from the edge of the salad bar. In Spanish he says, "My wife is picking me up. If your husband is not here when you get outside, sit with my wife in the car until he gets here, so you do not have to face the dangers by yourself." He walks around me and through the double swinging doors into the kitchen.

I stare after him, gratefully, even more so when I hear the voice boom over the heads of the patrons calling for a waiter again.

I grip the *palote*, preferring the *palote* I had brought from home over the rolling pin the kitchen provides. I imagine the *palote* flying across the room, and hear the clunk it makes as it bounces off the head of a customer. I would explain to the *gringos* that it's in my blood to throw things.

The tortilla sizzles as it is dropped on the hot grill. The second tortilla on the grill is flipped over, then the third is checked, and the fourth is placed in the styrofoam tortilla holder and set on the pass-through into the kitchen. As each container fills with a half-dozen hot *tortillas*, a waiter grabs it off the counter of the pass-through to put on the table.

Masa is rolled out. The three *tortillas* on the grill are flipped, and the warming holders are filled in a fluid sequence of motion. Hands move automatically. Sight and smell are the regulators. Mind in a trance. The doing is all there is.

The night finally eats up the time on the clock. I smile. I will make it through another night without quitting. Then I hear the words. I'm not certain if they are the words I thought I heard, so I listen carefully.

"Hot rocks, yeah. I'm telling you. It was a documentary or something. I don't remember exactly. But at home they cook those *tortillas* on hot rocks."

"Then it must be true."

I turn around and watch the two white-haired ladies pile veggies onto their plates. They catch me looking at them and they wave as they go to their table.

I grab my *palote* and sacrifice the last *bolita de masa*, rolling it to a too-thin consistency so that it tears when I lift it. I drop it into the trash on the way to the locker room.

After being in front of the grill for eight hours, flipping *tortillas* and rolling *masa*, the smell of the food is lost to the nose. But the fragrance that entices hungry customers to order more than what they can eat is the same smell that sticks for hours after work.

The smell is in the hair, on the clothes, even on the skin. The *masa* is under the fingernails; the hairs in the nose are white from the flour. A thin layer of grease from the grill covers the skin.

The art of making *tortillas* is taught. Women were making *tortillas* for the conquistadors from Spain in ancient times. The secrets, the skills, the basic ingredients are handed down from one generation of women to the next. These skills know no borders, no state lines, no international boundaries.

There is a loud crash as the locker room door bounces open against the wall. "Everybody in here. Out! Now!"

Still barefoot, I fear a fire and reach into the locker for my purse.

"Freeze. Let me see your hands."

Recognizing the tone of the voice, I raise my hands slowly above my head and turn around. In front of me stands a man with a crew-cut in a tan uniform, aiming a gun at me. "Get out here with the rest of them."

In the dining area, all the bus boys and cleaning crew are huddled together—everyone that is Latino. The rest of the employees are leaving through the front door after having their IDs checked.

A big man, very round around the chest, is bearing down on the oldest bus boy, a man of fifty. He was the one who had offered me safety in the parking lot. I heard that he has six children at home. I know he speaks English, just enough to tell a customer that he will get the waiter.

"He doesn't speak English," I interrupt the interrogation.

The uniformed man, his black hair shiny and slicked back off his forehead, rears his head up and approaches me. "Who are you?"

"Aura Morales. A U.S. citizen." I hold my head up proudly.

The thin man who pulled the gun on me in the locker room leaps to attention. "Lieutenant, I caught her hiding something in the lockers."

"Did you see what it was?"

"No, sir."

I would smile at the look the man gives to his subordinate, except I know how much trouble I am in. "I wasn't hiding anything. I thought there was a fire and I wanted to get my purse."

"Anybody ever tell you you talk too much?" He leans over me, his eyes as hard as pebbles in a shoe, his mouth a thin smile.

I want to say yes. I want to name all the people who have said those exact same words. But nobody else would laugh with me. This one can and might hurt me. I remain quiet but hold his stare.

"You know all these people?"

I look around. "Pretty much. Some just to say hello to."

"Tell me their names."

"Can't you ask 'em yourself?"

He takes me by the arm and yanks me in front of the men and points. "Start."

"*¿Tu nombre? por favor.*"

The grey-haired man bows his head. "Domingo Chávez."

"Ask him where he lives." The officer jostles me a bit to stay in command.

"*¿Donde vives?*"

"*Con mi hija en el barrio.*" Domingo keeps his eyes on the floor.

"He lives on the Westside with his daughter."

"How long has he been here?"

"*¿Que tanto tiempo tienes aquí?*"

Domingo hesitates then answers, "*No más de un año.*" No more than a year.

"He's been here all his life."

The officer shoves me back into the group, making me stumble. "I understand enough to know '*un año*' means one year." He signals to his troops. "Take 'em all in. We'll question 'em at the station."

I step up to him. "Wait. I can prove I am an American citizen."

"Yeah."

"In my purse. I carry my birth certificate with me. But it's in my purse."

"You expect me to believe something that you can purchase at any corner in the barrio? Take her along with the rest." He turns his back on me.

"But my children are expecting me home soon."

"You should have thought of that before you had so many that you lose track of them." He walks away.

Along with the rest of the men, I am herded outside to a gray van. The windows on the back doors are covered with criss-cross bars. The open doors click shut after we are all crammed inside. The van reeks of vomit and sweat. A young man begins to cry. An older man hushes him with a stern voice.

At the station, they stick me into a holding tank. The women, who were rounded up that night in their short skirts and sheer, skin-tight tops, check me over. I keep my hands loose at my sides and my chin level. I catch and hold for a few seconds the stare of each woman in the cell, then step into a corner, staring at the gray wall through the bars.

The painted gray bars of the cell sting my hands with their coldness. I reach out to a guard walking by. "Aren't we allowed one phone call?"

"You're heading back home. By tomorrow morning, you'll be eating *tortillas* with your family." He pats his generous stomach.

"But the phone call?" I speak to his retreating back.

"White bread and phone calls are for Americans." The door clangs shut, cutting off the light. All the women in the cell laugh.

I huddle in a corner, willing myself to disappear. The night is long, my bare feet cold.

Tortillas hold much food, wrapped around and tucked. They stay soft for a long time, unless they are left out, then they become hard, brittle. They can be reheated in the oven or over a flame. Always the taste is different.

The orange morning sneaks in the small window of the jail cell, pale and weak. I watch the sky, wearied and red-eyed, not having slept all night. My body aches from huddling in the corner. My feet are numb from the cold floor. And I'm hungry. A hot tortilla would taste good.

Two unfriendly officers bring breakfast which consists of sliced white bread, weak coffee, and runny eggs with no chili.

Several hours into the morning, the man from the night before and three other officers come and unlock the men's cell. They shout at the men, "All right, everybody in single file. Time to go back to Ole May-hee-co." The three officers laugh.

The older men follow the example of the younger men because some of them don't understand what is being said.

As they approach my cell, I reach out through the bars for the dark-haired man. "Please, let me call my family and let them know what's happening."

The man frowns, his thin smile disappearing, and brushes my hand off his arm. "We never allow calls to Mexico." He waves the other women back, and unlocks the door.

"I am American." I grip the bar. "I belong here."

The man points to the end of the line. "Step out or we'll come in and get you."

I scan the faces of the officers and see their excitement at the idea of my resisting them. I step out of the cell and follow the line out through the door. At the end of the hallway through the open doorway, we are being packed into a pale, green bus for the free trip back to Mexico.

As the landscape rushes pass, I refuse to cry. I refuse to let the guards see me cry. I sit by myself on the seat. Domingo Chávez sits on the seat ahead of me. Every time the guard walks by and stops near me, he swings his legs out into the aisle and watches him, steadily, unblinking, until the guard moves away. I nod thank you.

I stare out the window, waist-high grass swaying in the breeze. It will be a short trip, I know from the pleasure trips I took with my family. I stare out the window, each mile tearing me away. I stare out the window, the land flat and as far as my gaze can reach. I wonder who fixed my children breakfast this morning. I stare out the window, mountain range in the distance. Even the smells change as we move away from my home. I stare out the window. All I can see are the faces of my children and my husband.

A family meal is complete only with the cloth-covered bundle of tortillas passed from one person to another. Each diner takes a tortilla, uses it to scoop food, or to eat rolled up with butter. The mother stands at the stove, making sure that the tortillas are hot and fresh and plentiful for her family.

Tortillas, one constant since the time of Aztec Kings. The one memory every Latino child carries into adulthood is that of a woman in the family cooking tortillas. Tradition. A staple. Familiar as a mother's goodnight kiss.

⁓

I flag the air in front of my face with my hand to swat off the mosquitoes. They are buzzing a melody against the black quilt of the night. I peel away from the back of the lawn chair. The wide, plastic webs stick to my sweaty back.

Luz stands beside me, brush gripped in both hands, starting with eyes full of tears. "Did they bring you back?"

"Hitchhiked. An Indian family picked me up. After they heard my story, they brought me all the way home. I rode in the back of their pick-up with the children. They said they understood what it meant to be taken from your home." I touch the brim of my hat. "The eldest gave me his hat after he put the dream catcher on it."

Luz sits on my lap and snuggles against my stomach. "Do you think I can wear your hat to the spelling bee next weekend?"

"*Chulita*, you have all you need already here." I tap her head. "You already have all the answers you will ever need here." I put my hand over her heart. "You are a woman. You will be the best. That is all anyone can ask."

Luz talks into my chest. "So many people will be disappointed if I lose."

I put my hand under her chin and raise her face to me. "Then let them do it. Lots of people talk, but very few stand up in front of everybody and do what has to be done. You have the courage to show up. That's what counts."

Luz blinks back at me and opens her mouth when we hear her mother's words from the darkness. "It's getting late." Luz's mother fans the air in front of her face. "There are too many mosquitos out here."

Luz wipes the tears from her eyes with the back of her hand, gets up, and stands next to her mother. "*Abuelita* was helping me with my spelling."

"*¿Cómo?*" She looks at me, then eyes the empty glass of tequila on the table. "It's late. Time to go to bed." She kisses the top of her daughter's head and shepherds her back to the house with an arm around her shoulders.

I trail after them. At the door of the house, Luz looks over her shoulder back at me. "Thanks, *Abuelita*, for teaching me." She winks and laughs as she runs into the house to her bedroom.

My daughter stares after her daughter then looks at me. I smile, the *cigarillo* dipping. She throws up her hands in surrender and follows Luz.

I puff on the *cigarillo*. Through a blue haze of smoke, I look up at the sky, touch the brim of my flat-brimmed hat, and nod thank you.

Basic Ingredients

Bad memories spill out from the back of your head, starch your neck muscles, and poison your whole day. Good memories sneak around your ears and tug the corners of your mouth into a smile. Angry memories can drive you crazy for a lifetime.

Mrs. Emily Thatcher and Mrs. Helen Mendoza supervised the students rearranging the chairs in the cafeteria. "I don't think we'll need more than twenty-five chairs or so. What do you think, Helen?"

Helen Mendoza surveyed the room and chuckled. "Maybe a few more, just in case."

Tonight the school board would rule on whether the runner-up, Debbie Whitting, would represent the school at San Antonio's All-Star Spelling Contest since Luz Ríos had been accused of stealing the list of words used at the competition. Helen observed Emily setting up one more row of chairs and thought, you don't know Mexicans much.

Helen knew, without a doubt, that not only Luz's family would be there tonight, but so would every relative and friend within the school district. She dreaded the outcome. Somehow calamities were always made worse by the dramatics of Latinos. She sighed. She was intent on remaining divorced from their antics.

Emily counted rows of chairs as she walked towards Helen. Emily was a painter's chart of yellows with lemon-colored hair shagged down past her shoulders; a mustard linen suit, a white blouse with a huge, limp bow at her throat. Helen organized her wardrobe with precision—light brown hair combed in a smooth pageboy, deep blue blazer with a matching straight skirt tailored to fit, white blouse, beige stockings, and matching blue pumps. She had absorbed every dress-for-success book, magazine and manual there was.

"There. That should be enough. This is not a regular meeting, so we shouldn't expect a big turnout." Mrs. Thatcher smiled a Sunday-school-teacher smile.

Several hours later, Mrs. Thatcher was running amok. She corraled the young children who were attending the PTA meeting with their parents to assist in setting up more chairs. Over fifty people were in the room and more were streaming in.

At the left of the table where the school board sat, Helen positioned herself with a bird's-eye view of the front row. Luz's parents, Rubén and Rosaura, sat next to the middle aisle. Rosaura was pale but somber, dark eyes darker, short black hair combed smoothly, looking every bit like royalty in a fuchsia sheath dress, fitted to reveal a slim figure. Helen envied her luxury of never having to worry about weight. Luz sat next to them, appearing frightened but holding her head high.

Behind Luz sat Justina and their friends, Sofia Cuellar, Diana Ortiz, and her own daughter, Sally Jane. She had asked Sally Jane to sit with Tiffany and her mother, Mrs. Thatcher and Mrs. Whitting. But of course, that girl had a mind of her own. When Sally Jane had asked why, Helen had expressed her fears and sure enough, there she was, sitting in the same row as Luz and her parents.

Mrs. Manela Cuellar and Mrs. Marieta Ortiz and their husbands, Ramon and Vicente, nodded and waved to several people in the audience as they took their seats. Manela was in full regalia—hair whipped on top of her head with curls falling around her face, huge gold loop earrings, face masked in model-beautiful make-up, wraparound dress sticking to the parts that stuck out, fingernails long and red. Marieta had come prepared for battle—black hair coiffured in executive style, black suit, with a simple gold brooch pinned to her jacket. Her nails were also long and red. Helen figured Manela and Marieta had gone to the same nail shop together.

She remembered a time when the four of them, Manela, Rosaura, Marieta and herself, had hung together in grade school. Those had been fun times. Occasionally, she missed their talks. The other three had accused them of being foolish. But while Manela and Marieta talked about revolution and Rosaura covered herself with paint from her artwork, Helen had learned early how the system worked and who the system benefitted. Taught well by her mother, Helen acknowledged the advantages of being light-skinned. If any of them had been as light-skinned as she, they would have been motivated to surpass their surroundings, too.

Marieta waved at her. Helen turned to hear what the principal had to say as he hit the gavel on the table. "I wasn't expecting such a crowd. We have gathered here to discuss a simple matter."

Manela said loud enough for many to hear, "Not as simple as you."

Rosaura and Marieta took one of her hands and held it. Manela slumped back in her seat, subdued.

Helen didn't look in their direction, but paid close attention to the recitation of rules that had been violated and the justified consequences. Helen gripped the edge of the table when Rosaura stood and walked to the center of the middle aisle. "I wish to be heard."

There was a buzz of commotion as Mrs. Thatcher found the stand for a microphone. The mike was positioned in front of the table where the school board members sat. The President cleared his throat. "We'll have open mike for comments before we vote." He nodded at Rosaura.

Rosaura stretched on tiptoes to speak into the mike. "Who accuses my daughter? Why don't they show their faces?"

"The person who reported seeing your daughter with the list of words before the competition is a student. We don't want the vindictiveness of others to cause undue suffering for the child."

"How far did you investigate this accusation?"

"We investigated as much as we deemed vital to our decision."

With those words, twenty people rose and formed a line behind Rosaura. Marieta and Manela were sixth and seventh in line.

"Sir, are you keeping the identity a secret because this student is white?"

"The student who stood up for honesty was a very responsible Hispanic."

A loud murmur rumbled through the audience. Her earrings swinging, Manela shook her head with her hands on her hips. "No way. Just no way."

Helen felt frustrated. She knew this was going to happen. None of these people knew enough to let the authorities just do their jobs. They had to turn everything into some kind of racial incident.

Manela stepped out of the line. "Elena, do something. Tell them they can't do this. We voted you on the school board to represent us."

The President leaned over to the gray-haired man sitting next to him and asked, "Who is this Elena she's speaking to?"

The gray-haired man pointed down the table. "Helen Mendoza. It's how they say her name in their language."

Helen wanted to crawl under the table. She stared at the President with a smile glued to her face. He said, "All questions must be directed to the podium."

Manela glared at Helen. Marieta tugged her back into line, whispering into her ear. Manela shook her head and pointed a fist at Helen. Helen felt relief when Mrs. Thatcher motioned to her from the back of the room.

Agitated, Mrs. Thatcher whispered, "A little one is lost." Helen followed Mrs. Thatcher into the hallway.

Mrs. Thatcher fanned herself with an open hand. "By God, these people have so many children they keep losing them."

Helen hated the "they" word. She hated being lumped into a pigeonhole. "Tell me what happened."

"This young girl," Mrs. Thatcher pointed at an eight-year-old standing alongside of the wall, twisting her skirt around her fingers, "was supposed to be watching her baby brother. Instead she was distracted by her playmates and now they want to go racing through the building hunting for him."

Helen smiled at the young girl, then to Mrs. Thatcher she said, "You go down this hallway and I'll go the other way. A toddler wouldn't have gone far."

Helen walked down the hallway, trying all the doors. Finding one door unlocked, she stepped into the room. The smell of chalk filled her memory.

Helen remembered her mother pin-curling her hair every night so she would go to grade school with bouncing curls just like the other girls. Her new uniform was always pressed neatly. Young relatives, who didn't have as much as they did, received her faded uniforms.

Reaching for a piece of chalk, Helen observed she was standing in the science lab. School projects had been a family affair. A topographical map of the

United States had developed into a major production with plaster-of-Paris landscapes and food-colored plains and mountain ranges. Telegraph keys with shiny nails and wire that ran across the length of the room earned her the teacher's approval.

"Mrs. Mendoza, we found the child. He wandered back to his mother. Isn't that funny?" Helen nodded. "Are you coming?"

"I'll be right there."

Helen jiggled the piece of chalk in her hand like dice while she reminisced about her straight-A report cards through grade school and her honor-roll status in high school. Yet all of that had not been enough to spare her. After all her effort and the efforts of her parents, she was still one of those "they."

She remembered herself at twelve with her three girlfriends, Manela, Rosaura, and Marieta, and how they had commiserated with each other over every paramount life event or titanic tragedy. Nothing happened to one that the other three didn't hear about in detail.

On one spring Thursday, where only in San Antonio can the sun shine into closed eyelids, they had been excited about getting out of school. The school's baseball team was playing a game against the team from Alamo Heights. They had beaten them once before and ill feelings hovered on the breeze. The girls boasted of ripping the hair off the prissy cheerleaders from the Heights if they tried to get near their guys.

After lunch, their teacher, Sister Georgina, called the class to attention. She read off a list of names and asked those students to go to the nurse's station. Helen, her three *amigas*, and all the Chicanas in the class marched in twos and threes past the principal's office and into the reception area of the health clinic.

The nurse ordered them to sit alongside of the wall. The girls crowded around the three chairs. One by one, they were summoned into the inner office. And each girl left carrying a piece of paper, eyes on the floor, as she returned to the classroom.

Marieta and Manela squeezed her hands when her own name was called.

Helen swallowed hard as the nurse told her to get up on the examining table. She hid her hands under her skirt. She jerked her head away when the nurse attempted to slide a black plastic comb through Helen's hair.

"Be still. I have to check." The nurse grabbed a chunk of Helen's hair. "Hygiene is a value one should be taught at home. It's a miracle this doesn't happen more often." The nurse pulled the hair away from her scalp.

Helen grimaced.

The nurse peered for about three seconds and murmured, "Mm-huh."

As the nurse dropped the comb in a pan of alcohol, she said, while wiping her hands, "You are excused from school. Take this note home. Tell your mother to wash your hair in this Pine Tar shampoo. Then she'll have to pick the lice out one by one. You're not allowed back in school until I've had a chance to check your head. You understand?" She finally looked at Helen.

Helen nodded, her head arched high.

The nurse frowned and shouted, "Your parents. Can they read English? Talk it?"

Helen didn't answer.

"Will they be able to carry out these instructions? You know it's very important they do this right. If not, another epidemic will happen."

Helen reached out to take the note from the nurse.

The nurse pulled the piece of paper back from her. "You understanding me? You do talkie English, no?"

Helen snatched the note from the nurse's hand and stomped out. She passed her girlfriends without looking at them and walked back to her classroom.

As she gathered her books, the students whispered and giggled as one Chicana after another left the room. As Helen reached the door, she heard Sister Georgina announce, "There will be no school tomorrow. Your parents will be notified and we're asking them to make an appointment with your doctors. There is no need for alarm, as I'm sure this incident is confined to a select few. But since you all have been in the same room, it won't hurt to check." Sister Georgina smiled at all the seated girls.

The special shampoo had been a purple gook that had smelled badly and stained her skin and took a week to wash out the odor. Her mother had checked. She found none. Not a single one.

The chalk in Helen's hand broke in half. She picked up the small pieces from the floor and threw them into the wastebasket. She slapped one hand against the other and the chalk dust made her nose tingle. She drew a hanky from her skirt pocket and put it to her face when she heard, "We did it for Luz." She smothered her sneeze.

She sneaked to the open door, put her hand on the doorknob, and stole a glimpse through the slit between the door and the wall.

"Olga, this has gotten out of hand. You got to go tell them."

"You gone ballistic, girl. There's no way I'm going out in front of that crowd and tell them I made up this whole thing. You think I got a death wish or something?"

"*Mira*, this doesn't feel right. Luz did her best. She's one of us. We shouldn't be trying to mess it up for her."

Olga answered, "They would have shot her down anyway."

"Man, she's my friend. She wouldn't listen to us at the party when we told her not to do it. I just don't want her getting hurt."

Olga nodded, remembering the conversation.

Then Olga said, "Besides, everybody's treating her like she's César Chávez or something."

"I know. I know."

"*¡Órale!* Besides, you know what Debbie and her gang would do to Luz if she won. You were worried about her, too."

"*Sí, ¿comó no?*" Ana nodded vigorously.

"So I had to tell the principal that Luz had cheated. You thought it was a good idea too. Don't tell me different."

"*¡Híjole!* Don't get me in this. I didn't have anything to do with you telling. That's your claim, not mine."

Helen stepped through the doorway. The girls jumped. "Looks to me like you girls have some talking to do. We better hurry before they turn off the mike."

Ana cast her green eyes down the hallway searching for a possible escape route; her black hair was tied back with a green ribbon. Olga's brown eyes were wide with shock. She brushed her cheek with long, rhinestone-studded fingernails, the curls from her hairdo bouncing as she said, "Mrs. Mendoza, we have to go check on my baby brother." She wheeled in the opposite direction.

Mrs. Mendoza seized her arm. "Not so fast, *chiquita*. We've got some things to clear up first."

Olga yanked away and ran down the hallway. Helen raced after her and, sliding on the wax floor, banged into Olga, pinning her against the lockers. Ana covered her mouth in surprise as she watched Mrs. Mendoza take hold of Olga's arm.

"Do I drag you in, or are you going to walk in on your own?" Helen said.

Ana tiptoed away from the struggle.

"Stop." Ana took another step. "Don't make me come after you," threatened Helen.

Stunned, Ana spun around and moved closer to them.

They trudged down the hallway, Helen bringing up the rear. At the door of the cafeteria, Ana and Olga turned around. "Mrs. Mendoza, we didn't mean anything..."

Helen pointed to the door.

Olga, not one for giving in easily, pleaded, "But I was..."

Helen's face darkened and she squeezed into them; their shoulders squared against the door. Their faces were gray with anxiety. "Go in. Now," Mrs. Mendoza said softly.

Mrs. Whitting was at the mike, tears running down her face, saying, "This whole situation has been very traumatic for my daughter."

Manela, Rosaura, and Marieta stood to the side. Luz watched, poised and steady. People were mostly standing. Comments were shooting across the room: "Your girl's happy about it." "She's the one that probably caused all this."

Manela approached Mrs. Whitting. "Can you prove your daughter wasn't the one that told these lies about Luz?"

"My daughter doesn't lie." Mrs. Whitting's hand shook.

"Your daughter never wanted Luz to go." Manela was a storm brewing.

Helen recognized the danger signals as did Rosaura and Marieta. But to everyone's amazement, Rosaura stepped ahead of Manela. "I call for a run-off. Let your daughter and mine go at it again with new words." Rosaura covered the mike with her hand.

Helen could see Rosaura's mouth move, then Mrs. Whitting paled and swayed and reached behind her for someone to hold her up. Helen gripped both girls by their arms and forced them through the crowd in the aisle. "I have someone that has something to say," she yelled, but no one heard her.

The speaker pounded the gavel, but the sound was absorbed by the shouting.

Helen drove the girls closer to the front of the room, using them to move the crowd out of the way. She shouted again. "I have a speaker here."

Slowly, the girls attempted to slide back, but the tension behind them propelled them forward.

Mrs. Fuentes and Mrs. Tijerina gasped as they saw their granddaughters being marched to the front of the room. Luz's *abuelita* patted the two women's heavily-veined hands when Helen broke through the crowd.

"If you will be quiet for just a moment..." No one paid any attention to her. Manela was moving in on Mrs. Whitting, her hands raised in fists. Her husband reached for her to hold her back.

Marieta caught Helen's frantic look. Helen winked at her and mouthed words. Marieta put her index fingers in her mouth and whistled an ear-splitting sound that silenced all but the hard-of-hearing.

Into the silence, Helen announced, "I have someone who would like to say something."

The President stood, staring at Mrs. Mendoza. Manela scowled at her old homegirl. Rosaura's mouth dropped open as she viewed the polished and sophisticated woman who was standing with her blouse hanging out of her skirt, her hair sticking out in tufts, and the brightest grin on her face.

Olga felt the heat from Mrs. Mendoza's breath on her neck and slowly moved up to the mike. "I, uh, I..."

Helen shoved Ana beside her. "You shouldn't be alone. Homegirls stick together." Helen winked at Manela. Manela gawked at her old friend.

The president leaned forward. "You don't have to speak here. You can see me privately in my office tomorrow."

Olga nodded and stepped back, bumping into Mrs. Mendoza. "I, uh, I want to speak now."

The room had grown quiet; even babies weren't crying. Children had stopped playing, watching their parents for a signal. All eyes were on the young girls in the front of the room.

When nothing else happened, the president said, "This is too delicate a matter to be aired in the open like this. I insist that I see you in the morning."

Luz stared at her friends, puzzled. Olga looked past Ana and caught Luz's eyes for a second, then switched her gaze onto the floor.

Mrs. Mendoza spoke over the girls' heads. "As a board member, voted to represent my constituency," she nodded at Manela, "I insist that we hear what this young woman has to say now. Do we need to take a vote on it?"

The six board members sitting at the table looked to the president for direction. The president swallowed. "I believe that this matter will be served better if dealt with in the clear light of the morning. I want the girl to have the chance to know what trouble she may be getting herself into. I wouldn't want anyone being railroaded into anything." The president cast a stern look upon Helen.

Rosaura spoke out. "You're worried about harming this young woman, but it's okay to damage my daughter?"

The murmurs in the audience increased in volume.

The president pounded the gavel. "Silence. No one is attempting to maltreat anybody. The purpose of this meeting is to uncover any evidence that will absolve your daughter of any misconduct."

"Good," said Helen. "This young woman would like to speak to that issue at this time." She nudged Olga from behind.

With her head hanging, Olga said, "I just want to say that I made up the story I told you."

The president leaned so far forward that he appeared to be falling over the table. "Child, I couldn't hear you. Let's talk in the morning when you're feeling better."

Olga looked up, took a deep breath, and said clearly, "I made up the story I told you."

The president bounced back, ramrod-straight. "You mean Luz Ríos didn't steal the list of words before the competition as you said?"

"No, sir." Olga sneaked a glimpse at her grandmother over her shoulder. Mrs. Tijerina was running the beads of her rosary through her fingers, her lips moving in prayer.

Mrs. Whitting gasped, one hand covering her mouth, the other hand reaching for her daughter. "Oh, no."

The three *comadres* shifted their gaze upon Olga, changing from puzzlement to astonishment to anger and back to curiosity.

The president glared. "Did anyone put you up to this, child?"

Olga shook her head.

The president repeated his words with a deeper intensity, throwing a glare at Helen. "Are you sure?"

Olga's chin dropped to her chest. "Yes, sir, I'm sure."

"I want you in my office first period tomorrow morning." The president banged the table with his gavel. "The charges against Luz Ríos are now dismissed and this meeting is adjourned."

Mrs. Whitting escorted her weeping daughter out of the room. Mrs. Thatcher followed Mrs. Whitting, clucking after them, but looked back just enough to smile at Helen. Ana's and Olga's grandmothers, with their granddaughters in tow, walked straight-backed and proud out of the room; everyone parted for them to pass.

The room filled with shouts, laughter and tears. Uncles said, "We knew it all along." Aunts, "Luz would never do such a thing." Cousins, "*Andale*, about time one of us got a break." And friends, "We never lost faith in that girl." They hugged Luz and each other. Children clapped their hands, looking around for the reason their parents were so happy. Babies cried; toddlers jumped up and down. Little boys ran and slid across the shiny floor while mothers looked the other way. Little girls grinned and hung arms over each other's shoulders. Friends invited each other to their homes for a victory celebration.

Aura touched the rosary beads to her lips then slipped them into her pocket as her son-in-law approached. Rubén ushered Rosaura's mother to the front of the room. Aura kissed her granddaughter on the forehead then hugged Helen. "You do good. Both of you." Aura tolerated being escorted out of the jostling, cheering crowd.

The four old school chums squared off. Rosaura squeezed Helen's arm. "I'm so glad. Thank you."

"Didn't think you had it in you," said Manela.

"I knew you'd always come through in a pinch," put in Marieta, attempting to take the sting out of Manela's words.

"Not too bad for a homegirl, eh?" Helen grinned, feeling the best she had in a long time.

"Not too bad for a coconut," sneered Manela.

"*Andale*, watch what you call me, or I be taking you outside." With one hand on her left hip, Helen pitched it forward, the other hand in the air, finger pointed at her friend.

Sally Jane stood, eyes as big as the earring loops Manela wore, hands limp at her side, mouth open. Sofia, Diana, and Justina looked from Sally Jane to her mother and back to Sally Jane.

Manela grinned. "Aw right, homegirl." They slapped palms in mid-air.

Helen turned to Rosaura. "What did you say that turned poor Mrs. Whitting so pale?"

"Nothing, really." She smiled sweetly, holding one hand on top of the other at her waist.

Helen looked at Manela and Marieta for the answer. "We didn't hear anything. We were too far back."

Luz stepped into the middle of the group. "I heard." Tilting her head back and swinging it around to see everyone, she said, "*Mamá* told the lady that if she ruined my life, *Mamá* was going to ruin her face." Luz's grin stretched her face shiny.

The women leaned on each other laughing so hard. Holding her side, Manela said, "Girlfriend, if she only knew how much of a wimp you really are. Almost as much of a wimp as this one." She pointed at Helen.

Helen shrugged and spread her hands in front of her. "*Ay.* One of the few times the stereotype worked for us."

Time To Rise

Feliz Navidad. Cinco de Mayo. Día de Los Muertos. The morning feels like a bundling together of excitement from all the holidays of the year. Luz buries her face in her pillow, hearing movement in the kitchen, not wanting to get up and face this special day.

The phone rings. She can hear her mother's muffled voice speaking in the living room. Her father is walking back and forth down the hallway from the kitchen to their bedroom, checking with her mother. Is this the right shirt? The right tie? Where are my black socks? Did you get my suit from the cleaners? I was supposed to! *iHíjole!* Are they open on Sunday?

Her eight-year-old brother opens the door and gropes in front of him with one hand holding his pajama bottoms tight. "One more door," she tells him. With eyes still shut, he stumbles out, one hand outstretched in front of him, and she hears him opening the bathroom door.

Her sister burrows deeper into her bed, but soon the smell of fresh *tortillas* and *barbacoa* rouses her to lift her head from the pillow. "Why is everybody up?" She squints in her sister's direction. "Oh yeah. Your day." She drops back onto her pillow.

Luz smiles. Her day. The day she has been looking forward to for two weeks now. The day she thought would never get here. Now that it has, she isn't so sure she is glad. The day she will compete. Compete and win. Or compete and lose. Her stomach twists. She grips the sheet and the spasm passes.

She and her family drove by the auditorium. The place looked huge. Bigger than she had thought. Her stomach twists again.

She doesn't want to think about how one of her friends, Ana, almost ruined her chances of going. Her stomach cramps and she runs for the bathroom. She holds herself over the toilet bowl as a flood of mess erupts from her.

Hearing the commotion, her mother rushes in and rubs her back. After her daughter is done, she wipes Luz's face with a wet cloth. "Nervous stomach?"

Luz shakes her head, noticing that her mother has already fixed her brown eyes with make-up and her black hair is pulled back with a handpainted, wooden hair comb.

Mrs. Ríos smiles as she sits on the edge of the tub. "I remember one time when..."

"*Mamá*, please, no when-I-was-your-age stories *ahorita*."

Rosaura Ríos notes the bit of green in her daughter's usually milk chocolate complexion and decides the story isn't that important anyway. She hugs her daughter, feeling the smallness of Luz's fourteen-year-old body with her arm, the throbbing of Luz's heart under her hand, and strokes her sleep-mussed black hair.

Luz leans against her mother, feeling secure for the moment, and asks, "Do I have to go?"

Rosaura smiles into her daughter's hair. "No."

Luz pulls back and looks at her mother. "Very funny. Ha, ha." She crosses her eyes.

"Your father went out early this morning and got you your favorite breakfast."

At the mention of food, Luz leans over the toilet again. But everything remains where it belongs.

"Brush your teeth and come into the kitchen. I'll wake your sleepy sister."

In the kitchen, a stack of hot corn tortillas towers beside a foil-covered dish full of barbacoa which sits in the middle of the table. Luz plops herself in her usual place. Her father exchanges knock-knock jokes with her brother, and her mother feeds the baby. Her *abuelita* hustles from one end of the kitchen to the other, preparing food for the big party after the competition. Her sister, Justina, stares at her plate with eyebrows arched high, attempting to keep her eyelids open.

There is a knock on the back door. *Tía* Gloria, her mother's sister-in-law, hobbles in. She takes the chair Rosaura offers and hands her the crutches. "*Gracias,* Rosaura." Grey-streaked hair, *Tía* Gloria lost one leg from below the knee to diabetes. "You must be anxious to get to the competition already, Luz?"

Luz covers her mouth with her hand.

All morning long, cousins, aunts, uncles, friends of Luz's father at work, friends of her mother and artists her mother knows come by to wish Luz luck. The competition is at three that afternoon and everyone promises to be there. Luz thinks, maybe it's a good thing that the auditorium is so big.

Luz approaches her *abuelita* while the rest of the family is fighting over the bathroom. "*Abuelita*, have you thought about it?" She has convinced herself that if she can wear her grandmother's hat, the contest will go her way.

Aura's long braid hangs down her back from underneath a black felt reservation hat with a beaded hatband. Her face sorts into a questioning gaze, the thousands of wrinkles crossing each other in a maze pattern. She is covering dishes with foil as she looks down at her granddaughter. "Thought about what?" The dream catcher attached to the hatband swings with the movement.

"Can I wear your hat at the competition? I know it will bring me luck."

"*Ay, mija,* I've told you, luck you don't need. You have it all here." She taps the side of the girl's head with a finger then places a hand over her heart. "The winning or the losing is not important."

"That's what you think." With arms back, elbows on the counter, Luz slumps, stretching her legs in front of her.

"You will win because you show up. The courage to do the thing is what makes you a winner."

Luz digs the floor with the toe of her slipper. "You don't have to show your face at school on Monday."

Aura strokes her granddaughter's cheek. "Your face is the face I love to look at on any day."

There is a knock at the back door. Luz opens it. Rosaura's best friend, Mrs. Helen Mendoza and her daughter, Sally Jane, enter, arms laden with platters of food. Mrs. Mendoza dons an apron over her white suit and immediately begins to help Aura in the kitchen. Her hair is pulled back into a bun, her face smooth, her smile huge, her eyes soft and pretty with light make-up. Sally Jane quickly slips out to join her friends before her mother can lasso her into a kitchen job.

About noon, Mrs. Manela Cuellar bursts into the house, wearing a purple coat-dress that fits tightly on all the parts that Luz's mother won't let her show. Mrs. Marieta Ortiz trails right behind her in a sleeveless, red-and-yellow-flowered dress with a gathered skirt. Both have gigantic totebags hanging off their shoulders. Their daughters, Sofia and Diana, sneak off with Sally Jane to Justina's bedroom. Luz hears laughter and loud voices in the kitchen as she combs her hair in the bathroom. Laughter and loud voices are a part of being around Mrs. Cuellar and Mrs. Ortíz.

Luz slowly lowers her comb when through the mirror she sees her mother and her mother's best friends fill the doorway.

Long, red fingernails point at Luz. "*Ay, mira, que chula.* Rosaura, you can't expect your daughter to go in front of all those people looking like that?" Mrs. Cuellar waves her hands in front of the other people's faces in the congested doorway. She has a mask of make-up that is New York model perfect, her smooth skin smoother, her eyes dazzling, her arched brows darker, her full lips mauve. "She's a beautiful girl. You have to let me expose her inner beauty."

Mrs. Ortíz nods in agreement. "Rosaura, you want those other girls showing your daughter up?" Her brown eyes are lined and highlighted; her lips are also mauve.

Rosaura sighs, knowing it's impossible to fight these two when they get an idea into their heads. "I'll let you do her hair, but no make-up."

The two women grin.

Rosaura Ríos cocks her head at her best friend. "Manela?"

"Of course." Mrs. Cuellar sticks her hand up in the air in a solemn pledge.

"Marieta?"

"Wouldn't hear of it." Mrs. Ortíz raises her hand too.

⎯⎯⎯⎯⎯

Luz sits in front of the mirror Mrs. Ortíz has hauled in from Luz's mother's bedroom and that Mrs. Cuellar has propped up on Luz's desk. Justina, Sofia, Sally Jane and Diana hover in the background, spying on the craft. Luz watches Mrs. Cuellar brush her hair into high fashion curls on top of her head. Rosaura sticks her head in the doorway. "*Ay*, Manela, she's only fourteen."

"Okay, okay." Mrs. Cuellar lets the hair drop, hitting Luz's shoulder, curling under. "But I'm just going to pull it off her face a little."

Rosaura opens her mouth.

"Just enough to show her beautiful face."

Rosaura shakes her head and retreats to her own bedroom with Helen.

Mrs. Cuellar and Mrs. Ortíz grin at each other. "Now."

Marieta dumps the big bag she has been carrying onto the top of the desk. What looks like a thousand different colors of lipsticks, fifteen cases of eye shadow in rainbow colors, six eyeliner pencils, five tubes of mascara, four different colors of base, three compacts, two powder puffs, a bag of cotton puffs, and tweezers scatter across the desk. Marieta takes from her bag a hair blower, a curling iron, pink foam rollers, two packages of bobby-pins, one brown, the other black, and three cans of hair spray. She points and says, "*Órale*, you guys sit on the bed." The four young girls sit in a row. Marieta smirks. A rare time when orders don't have to be repeated.

With quick strokes and tongue-pinched-between-lips concentration, Marieta powders, lines, and colors the girls' faces. She bends and her black hair falls across one cheek, the other side combed behind the ear. "You're young girls so you don't need much. But it never hurts to start learning about these things," says Marieta as she shapes Sofia's eyebrows with a tiny brow-brush.

Manela smiles in the mirror while she duplicates the effort on Luz. "Of course, it's always good to help nature. Do you think I wake up looking this beautiful?" She pats her black hair, piled on top of her head with curls falling around her face.

Luz nods.

From behind, Manela hugs her around the shoulders. "Such a child. I have so much to teach you."

Marieta grins. "Just don't tell your mother."

"*Ay*, I remember that mother of yours," Manela shakes her head as she wraps a strand of Luz's hair around the curling iron. "She was a wild one, that's for sure."

Justina and Luz swap looks of curiosity. "Like how?" asks Luz.

"She was so popular. Her phone never stopped ringing."

Marieta adds, "The boys would come up to us but all they wanted was to talk about your mother. Would we introduce them to her? What kind of flowers did she like? What could they do to win her heart?"

"And if one of them was rejected by her or they saw her out with another guy," Manela nods at Marieta, "which was all the time—they would come running to us. They would cry on our shoulders. Talk about her for hours. Some even threaten to kill themselves if she didn't go out with them."

Justina leans forward on the edge of the bed. Marieta gently puts her hand under the girl's chin and closes her mouth.

Marieta pouts. "We were very depressed. Boys never took us out to be with us. They only took us out because they thought it would get them closer to your mother."

"If they did take us out, all they did was ask us questions about your mother. We were very lonely." Manela flourishes the heated curling iron like a sword. Luz ducks.

Marieta lowers her voice. The girls perched on the edge of the bed arch toward her. "I remember at the Senior Prom, my date insisted that we go to all the same places that Rosaura and her date went. It was so embarrassing." She puts a hand to her heart. "He never even kissed me good night when he dropped me off. He was in too much of a hurry to get back to the car so the other guy wouldn't be alone with your mother."

"That's the truth, because me and my date were following behind them in his car. And I got home late and got into big-time trouble because of your mother." Manela shakes her head.

Luz turns her head and gapes at Manela. She coughs as she is hit in the face with a shot from the hair-spray. "What did she do?"

Manela twists the girl's head back facing forward and speaks to her in the mirror. "When her date walked her to her front door, my date parked his car in such a way that his headlights were shining on them. Jump the curb he did. Then he put on the high beams. Your mom and her date were in a spotlight. Like on American Bandstand."

Justina gulps. "Did she go in the house?"

Marieta laughs. "Nothing stopped your mother. You just wouldn't believe what she did."

Through the mirror, Luz shifts her eyes off Manela and pins them on Marieta. "Did she kiss the boy?"

"Nope."

"Nah. Nothing so simple." Manela checks the mirror for any lose strands of hair attempting to escape her.

Luz and Justina look at each other. "Then what?" They ask together.

Manela and Marieta grin at each other. "Well, maybe we've said too much already."

"No, no. We won't tell my mother. I promise." Luz crosses her heart. Justina does the same.

Manela looks at Marieta. "What do you think?"

"We've told them this much. It's our duty to tell them the rest. They should know the whole story about their mother."

"All right." Manela packs her totebag. "Your mother and her boyfriend..."

"Standing right in the spotlight..." stresses Marieta while she loads everything into her totebag.

"Of my boyfriend's high beams..." Manela taps her chest with the hairbrush.

"Started dancing."

"Started dancing, and dancing. She danced with her date until my boyfriend's car battery ran out. I couldn't get home on time and that's how your mother got me in trouble on our prom night."

Marieta checks the final product in the mirror. "We better go get your mother for her approval."

The two women walk out the bedroom door and stop just on the other side in the hallway.

Justina's friends start giggling. Luz looks at Justina. "Our mom got phone calls from guys?"

"And candy," adds Sally Jane.

"Our mom had guys after her?"

"Lots of guys," stresses Diana.

Together they say, "Our mother danced with a guy?"

"Until dawn," finishes Sofia.

With wide grins on their faces, Manela and Marieta slap a high five and continue down the hallway.

———

Luz spins in her full-length slip in the middle of the kitchen, surrounded by everyone, while her mother inspects Manela's handiwork.

"Well, I guess it's okay. You don't think she has on too much rouge?"

"Rosaura, she'll be on stage with all those lights shining on her. You don't want her looking sickly. Or worse yet, looking too pale."

The four young girls are giggling and staring at Rosaura.

She ignores them. "Turn around. I want to see the back of your head."

While twisting around, Luz fastens her eyes on her mother.

"Turn around, *mija*."

Sally Jane is whispering into her mother's ear.

Helen laughs out loud, then unsuccessfully smothers it with a hand.

Manela scowls at Sally Jane. Marieta hushes Helen. The four girls giggle louder.

"Would anybody care to clue me in on what's happening?" Rosaura searches the faces of everyone in the room.

All the females try to sober their expressions and fail miserably.

Luz touches her mother's hand. "Is it true that Mrs. Cuellar got into trouble on y'all's prom night because of you?"

Rosaura shoots Manela a look of remembered mischief. "Girlfriend, what have you been telling the girls?"

With hands up in the air, Manela pleads, "Not me. Marieta told them."

Rosaura twists around and spears Marieta with a look. "Give it up."

Marieta shakes her head and can't speak because she's laughing so hard.

The young girls watch their elders with disbelief.

Holding her sides, Helen tells her, "Remember the trouble on prom night?"

"Yeah, I was grounded for a month. What of it?"

"So it's true. You got my mom and their moms in trouble." Sally Jane is bouncing on one foot she is so excited.

"I got them into trouble." Rosaura wheels on Manela. "You got me in trouble that night and lots of other nights." Getting no response, she turns to her daughter, "What did they tell you?"

Luz clicks her mouth shut, then answers. "They said all the boys were after you."

Justina jumps in. "They said all the boys liked you better."

Sofia adds, "They told us how all the boys talked just about you."

Not to be left out, Diana says, "Like how all the boys threatened to kill themselves if you didn't go out with them."

Rosaura stares at her girlfriends then breaks out laughing.

Sally Jane, still bouncing, inserts, "How the guys were fighting with each other to be with you."

Smiling, Rosaura puts her hand on the back of her head and the other on her hip, striking a movie star pose. "Well, that part's true."

Helen grins. "Your father is the only guy your mother has ever..."

There is a knock on the door.

Looking away from Helen, Rosaura orders, "Luz, run and get a bathrobe on."

By the time Luz reenters the kitchen, there is silence. Her mother, Mrs. Cuellar, and Mrs. Ortíz lean against the kitchen counter. Mrs. Mendoza is standing next to the phone. The baby sits on the floor, playing with a rubber hammer. Justina, Sofia, Sally Jane, and Diana cluster together at one end of the table. On the other side of the table, Mrs. Fuentes and Mrs. Tijerina stand beside their granddaughters, Olga and Ana. Luz steps closer to her mother and Rosaura puts her arm on her daughter's shoulder.

Mrs. Fuentes, who only reaches the height of her granddaughter's shoulders, says, "We come to tell you something."

Mrs. Tijerina has her rosary in her hand and every time she moves, it jangles.

Ana clears her throat. "We came to wish you lots of luck."

Olga stays behind Ana. "We really want you to win today."

Ana nods. "We really do."

Manela leans against the kitchen counter. "If you really..."

Rosaura doesn't even look at her. "Manela, leave it alone. It's theirs to deal with."

No one says a word.

Rubén Ríos, Luz's father, steps into the kitchen. "Hey, is this party ever going to..." He takes in everyone's expression, does an about-face and flees the room.

Nudged by her grandmother, Olga steps forward. "Luz, I didn't want you to get hurt. I was afraid of what would happen if you won."

Manela snorts.

"I've talked to my grandmother and she took me to the priest and I talked about it to him. I guess I wanted to win the contest at South San just as much as you did. I just didn't have the guts you did to go for it. I guess I was too scared to want more. Something like that."

Aura, Luz's grandmother, walks into the kitchen. "Amparo. Consuelo. Hasn't anyone offered you a chair? You would think they were raised with no manners."

"*No, gracias*. We only come for a few minutes." Mrs. Tijerina taps Ana on her arm. "We go now. Let them have the happy time."

Rosaura reaches out. "Mrs. Tijerina, Mrs. Fuentes, can I offer you something to drink? Some food?"

"*No te molestes. Ya nos vamos.*"

"Can my husband take you home?"

"*Está bien.* Ana drive the car *de la hermana. Vente Hija.*" The two old women turn, heads high and backs proud.

Olga stops at the door and turns back to face them. "Be careful Luz. Those white girls don't like it."

Manela can't restrain herself. "Why should she watch out for them when she got friends like you?"

Luz steps forward. "If they do come after me, I expect you to be covering my back."

Olga hangs her head. "Thanks. I'll try."

Luz says, "No. You will."

Olga shrugs. "There's so many of them."

"You will."

Olga shrugs and nods at the same time, then turns and leaves.

Rosaura hugs her daughter.

Rubén walks in. "*Apurense.* Look at the time. You women yaking away, visiting, when we got a deadline to meet."

Marieta grins. "Just because you're the man, that makes you the official timekeeper?"

Manela spins him around by the shoulders and nudges him toward the door. "Go, go. Watch your football game or whatever other violent thing is on TV. Let the women handle the important things."

Rubén swings back around. "That's why I'm concerned about the time. You women have never been on time for anything in your lives."

"We'll show you." There's a mad exodus out of the kitchen into the bedrooms with yelling and hollering.

"Where's my dress?" Did anyone see my shoes?" "Who's been in my bag?"

Rubén winks at his mother-in-law. "Works every time."

As a family, Rubén, Rosaura, Ramón, Manela, Vicente, Marieta, Helen, Luz, Justina, Sofia, Diana, Sally Jane, *Tía* Gloria and Aura swarm into the backstage waiting room of the auditorium. Manela grabs the arm of a young man walking by in a dark suit with a name tag. "Who is the person in charge?"

He points to a woman with blonde hair cut short, wearing a pink suit. They shift course. As she spots them, she navigates in their direction with a smile on her face. "It's such a pleasure to meet you. Your being here early makes it convenient for everyone."

Rosaura whirls and faces her husband. "You said we were late."

Rubén grins, holding up his hands. "It worked. We're on time for once."

Manela slugs him on his shoulder. "*Cabrón.*"

The lady in the pink suit searches the faces of the young girls. "Which one is Luz?"

Luz is propelled in front of the family.

Sticking out her hand, the lady says, "Hi. My name is Mrs. Thompson. I'm so glad to meet you. I'm absolutely thrilled that you could be here today. It's a great honor to be representing your district. I'm sure you will do an outstanding job. You'll make your school and your family," she looks up and implies everyone present, "very proud today."

Luz feels her stomach heave.

Mrs. Thompson faces the band of family supporters. "Luz will be fine here. All of you are welcome to go into the auditorium and find your seats. There has been a section reserved for you. If you have any trouble, please notify me and I'll do whatever I can."

Rosaura leans forward to kiss her daughter good-bye.

"*Mamá*, please, not in front of everyone."

Rosaura pulls back. "Just a peck?"

Luz sighs and nods.

Rosaura hugs her daughter tightly, kisses Luz on the cheek, and wipes her eyes with a lace-edged hanky. Then everyone else in the group comes forward and kisses her. "Slaughter 'em out there," from Manela. "Remember. You're a winner," from Marieta. "No matter what happens, we love you," from her father. "Turd Face," from her sister.

Luz is relieved when the last of her family is escorted through the door by the patient Mrs. Thompson. She looks for a seat to wait out the time and she spots her grandmother, standing by herself near the entrance. Luz goes to her. "*Abuelita*, do you want me to walk you out where the others are?"

Aura swings her gaze back onto her granddaughter. "Everyone here," she waves her hand at all the contestants in the room, "not one looks as smart as you."

Luz smiles.

Aura sits down and pulls her granddaughter by the hand to the seat next to her. She studies Luz's eyes and takes off the black, felt reservation hat. She sets it on her lap.

Luz holds her breath. Maybe her *abuelita* has changed her mind and is going to let her wear the hat after all.

Aura fiddles with the dome of the hat then reaches toward Luz. Luz looks down and watches as her *abuelita* pins the dream catcher onto the front of her dress. "All you need is here." She taps the dream catcher which lays over her heart.

Luz hugs her grandmother. Mrs. Thompson clears her throat. "I'm sorry. No relatives are allowed backstage. May I escort you to your seat?"

Abuelita lets the pretty, pale lady lead her to join her family.

After the introductions, Luz takes her place in front of a microphone among those lined up along the edge of the stage. She scans the audience and her family waves. Manela holds up her hands clenched together over her head in triumph. The commentator asks for silence and begins the competition.

"Miss Ríos, will you please spell 'fuchsia'."

Luz looks somberly out into the audience. Her father takes her mother's hand and grips it tight. *Tía* Gloria leans over so Sofia can whisper the word the woman couldn't hear. Aura lowers the black, felt reservation hat over her eyes. Marieta squeezes her handbag. Helen stares at Luz trying to send her the answer telepathically. Manela shimmies to the edge of the seat ready to jump up and protest. Luz looks at her sister and winks. Then she breaks out in the biggest grin ever on a young girl's face.